To   Ian

C000301934

Only correct
A teacher slot

Simon

Simon Green

www.fast-print.net/store.php

ONLY CORRECT
Copyright © Simon Green 2011

All rights reserved

All characters are fictional. Any similarity to any actual person is purely coincidental

ISBN 978-184426-890-0

First published 2011 by
FASTPRINT PUBLISHING
Peterborough, England.

An environmentally friendly book printed and bound in England by
www.printondemand-worldwide.com

Mixed Sources

Product group from well-managed
forests, and other controlled sources
www.fsc.org Cert no. TT-COC-002641
© 1996 Forest Stewardship Council

PEFC Certified

This product is
from sustainably
managed forests
and controlled
sources

www.pefc.org

This book is made entirely of chain-of-custody materials

This book is dedicated to all teachers everywhere

Acknowledgements

I should like to thank the MCC for permission to quote from the website Laws of Cricket and Collins Education for permission to quote from the Collins Easy Learning German Grammar

Teachers are those people who help us to solve
problems that without them we would never have had

(A pupil, Friedrichshafen, Germany late 19th century)

This is a true story

Only some of the facts have been invented

Only correct

Introduction   1

Chapter 1: Singular or puerile   8

Chapter 2: Vorsprung durch Cricket   20

Chapter 3: Irritable vowel syndrome   38

Chapter 4: The speaking test: only correct   55

Chapter 5: Banda brothers   69

Chapter 6: The exchange trip – first leg: away   85

Chapter 7: Doing words and describing words   105

Chapter 8: New variant CPD   112

Chapter 9: Cover story   136

Chapter 10: Summertime   147

Only correct

Introduction

I am in TA.

That's not in *the* TA (Territorial Army) and I am not *a* TA (teaching assistant).

No. I am in TA.

Just like AA (but not *the* AA) or GA but certainly not like LA (Local Authority) or LA (Los Angeles). It is not like BA (Bachelor of Arts) or MA (Master of Arts) and has no connection at all with C&A (C&A) or Q&A (Question and Answer) or The R&A (The Royal and Ancient) or The V&A (Victoria and Albert).

But it may all end up being sweet FA.

I am a teacher.

It has been said: *once a Catholic, always a Catholic*. For even those who stray, relapse or recant, it is as difficult to rid oneself of Catholicity as it is to rid oneself of one's nationality, race or cultural identity. A sense of guilt pervades and it is surely no coincidence that the suffix following alco- and worka- to denote addiction also follows cat- to denote another kind of affliction.

It has been said: *once a teacher, always a teacher*. Like inborn religion, there is something about being a teacher that is more than the mere description of a profession. Teaching is so much bound up in the warp and weft of personality that to extricate the person from the job is like trying to separate the yolk from the egg, the gin from the G & T, or the custard from the trifle. It can be done but what remains is insipid, bland and unrecognisable.

A teacher's life is but one long multiple-choice question with no ambiguity and no uncertainty. Heisenberg for most teachers simply hadn't done his homework.

Question 1:

Teachers should:

a) Have complete respect from their pupils at all times
b) Entertain their pupils with witty banter and charming asides
c) Divert their pupils from anti-social behaviour towards model citizenship
d) Adapt to the needs (emotional, cognitive, financial) of their pupils

Answer: (a)

Question 2:

Pupils should

a) Obey their teachers at all times and without question and just do what they are told, is it so difficult for crying out loud, I have already explained that 17 times you just aren't listening sit still while I am talking to you why are you late don't take that tone of voice with me right I'll see you after the lesson get out get out get out
b) Ask intelligent questions from time to time
c) Display a modicum of motivation
d) Bring a pencil and paper to the lesson

Answer: (a)

Question 3:

Parents should

a) Not come to parents' evening if they don't have anything complimentary to say
b) Not do their children's homework
c) Not abuse their children's teachers
d) Ensure that their children get enough sleep, have a good breakfast, get them to school on time, make sure that they have the right equipment and all ingredients for cookery in a proper tin, wash the PE kit regularly, not complain about detentions, not call their children Thong or Piercing, not insist that their son opens the batting for the U13 XI just because they gave the team scorer a lift.

Answer: all the above.

Teachers have an obsessive-compulsive disorder that is displayed by a desire to correct. They cannot let things be, but have to rectify, to mark, to cure, to remedy, to rescue, to emend, to repair, to fix, to amend, to improve, to resolve and, above all, to put right. Whether this is a genetic disposition, an ingrained personality trait or learned behaviour is unclear. The jury is out and there is little research of any consequence on the matter. The fact remains, however, that when faced with error, teachers reach for the red pen.

Where normal people will let a grocer's apostrophe hang, they shudder in its presence and feel an urge to amend the offending script. Where others, through ignorance or inertia, will let the estate agent's offence regarding *accomodation* go, they feel obliged to pass comment. Where regular listeners to the radio will barely acknowledge an issue with *less people*, they fire off an email or letter to the papers bemoaning the fall in standards. Where others will listen cheerfully to a sports commentary, they grind their teeth in irritation at the mere mention of *the lads done good, he bowls real quick, he has took his chance.*

They are at the forefront of any debate about split infinitives, pronunciation of place names and mental arithmetic. Those of a certain age will remember wistfully box analysis, parsing and times table drilling.

Teachers can rarely enjoy a meal out. The menu will be riddled with errors of syntax, spelling, translation and punctuation. Instead of choosing a nice fruity red to accompany the steak, they will fixate on the impossibility of *panini's*, the grotesque mismatch of *soup de jour* or the misspelling of *apple stroodle*.

Merely walking down the street may bring on symptoms that can be characterised by nervous twitching upon seeing a newsstand. Is it not possible to write a headline of merely five words without making a mistake, a grammatical error, an infelicitous spelling?

Bus driver's demand less hours! Police seeks new grafitti vandals! Bishop blesses' new church bells'.

In company, they automatically and instinctively correct any date, capital city, longest river, shortest distance, Shakespearean quote, chemical formula or biological fact that has been wrongly attributed. Out of tact, this may well be carried out internally lest others take offence, but the correction will be made, explicitly or implicitly and the error simply cannot go unregarded. Ever alert to new forms of attack on the English language, scientific knowledge or historical understanding, teachers live in a state of perpetual readiness somewhat akin to *red alert.* They only have to lower their guard once and before they know it an Exocet of gross misunderstanding will have penetrated their defences.

How often must they endure *he did it off his own back, that is a mute point, all that glitters is not gold,* and *it went down like a damp squid* in silence, yearning to step in and yet fearful of reproach?

Many teachers are tired, not through lack of sleep, but as a result of total vigilance.

It is for this reason that teachers tend to marry teachers because many a first date has revealed a kindred spirit when encountering a menu. Both instinctively notice the nervous tic, the in-drawing of breath, the curl of the lip, the involuntary sigh when faced with *pain chocolate, chicken with noddles, ("oh, you too ... I thought I was the only one...")* and tales of such frustration quickly lead to a desire to spend more time in each other's company. Able to confess such fixations and free to confide an overwhelming urge to ameliorate at every opportunity, teachers make admirable soulmates. They can share conspiratorial glances when encountering the foibles of others and they can feel the illicit thrill of rightness the moment they encounter the vanities of the world at large.

Like most addictive obsessions, there is no cure, although counselling may be of some benefit. Bonding sessions with other sufferers are generally thought to provide some palliative relief and these usually occur in staff rooms at break or lunchtime. The sessions usually end when one teacher announces: "well, I can't stay here chatting all day, I've got piles of marking to do..."

and the others immediately take the hint and respond in kind: "yes, me too.." and leave the comparative safety of the staff room, their hands already trembling nervously towards the ubiquitous red pen.

I am in TA. Teachers Anonymous.

My name is Simon and I am a teacher.

Chapter 1

Singular or puerile

Teaching your first lesson is rather like losing your virginity – it can be over in a few brief moments or it can seem to last for ever; it can be remembered with wistful sighs or with heartfelt groans; it can be the start of a beautiful relationship or the start of a guerrilla war. One major difference is that one is normally carried out in secret, the other with an audience. One major similarity is that once past the experience, there is no going back.

Whilst some teachers claim to forget where they mislaid their virginity, none will ever forget their first lesson.

My first experience of teaching almost never happened.

In the early 1970s there seemed to be only two options for modern languages graduates: to teach or not to teach. I chose the first option, and that made all the difference.

Like many teachers of my generation (the baby-boomers) I had gone straight from school to university and was about to repeat the trick in reverse. This was well before the days of gap years and it was not uncommon to go directly from school to university to school without passing Life Outside at all. Travel to far-flung foreign climes was less common and even though I had spent a short period in France during my degree, it was not really long enough to make any serious impression on my spoken expertise. Because I was one of a new breed of undergraduates doing a variety of subjects, I had only been required to spend a month in France (and later a month in Germany). This was barely sufficient to be anything more than an extended holiday with occasional seminars thrown in to make the whole experience appear vaguely educational. My spoken French scarcely improved as I spent most of my time with fellow students and trying to avoid answering any questions at the seminars.

Following graduation, I had gone along to a PGCE (Postgraduate Certificate in Education) interview fresh faced and keen and assumed it would all be rather a formality. I had been taught French; I had learnt French; ergo, I wished to teach French. What could be more straightforward?

However, it was quite clear from the outset that the PGCE lecturers wanted to make sure that all that I had previously learnt was well and truly washed out of my system. They were also highly dubious about my level of French competence and insisted on a year in France to make sure that I knew the subject well enough to teach it.

This was in the heady days of stimulus/response methodology and language laboratories and the audio-visual method. Technology had infected all subjects, including modern languages. There was an almost naïve belief in a scientific approach to education. As far as modern languages went, speaking was the principal objective. Suffice it to say that boundless optimism and an unshakeable belief in American research with lab rats proved beyond any reasonable doubt that English pupils would soon be communicating effectively with anything within range, and what is more, in French.

So it was that still fresh faced and keen and with a desire eventually to order that bloody cup of coffee in Paris without becoming the laughing stock of every waiter around and descending into Peter Seller's special way of speaking French "'av you a ruuum?" I signed up with the Central Bureau for Educational Visits and Exchanges (known affectionately as the Central Bureau – sounding like a good front for Eastern European spies) and was duly assigned to a secondary school in the South of Brittany.

The intention was to brush up my French sufficiently so that I could return to the UK in order to inflict upon future generations of pupils the delights of French language and culture. The gap between hope and reality was soon to become evident.

A week before I was due to go I had a throbbing pain in one of my big toes and was referred to the casualty unit of the local hospital. The doctor was not in the least sympathetic and took just one look at the offending toe and said: "You will need to put these drops on your infected toe for three weeks and then come back and see me again." I twitched at the sound of the word "infected" and twitched again – like I did last summer – at the thought of coming back to see him in three weeks.

When I told him that I was about to go to France for a year and couldn't follow his instructions (plus inwardly wondering how on earth I would explain "in-growing toe-nail" in French if one mere cup of coffee was already proving a challenge), he said brightly:

"Oh well in that case it had better come off. And because most in-growing toenails also infect the other big toe, we might as well take off the other one at the same time." Let's twitch again.

Without further ado, he injected both big toes with a local anaesthetic and proceeded to cut off the toenail from each foot. Well, when I say cut, that does not really do justice to the procedure. The garden secateur-shaped implement dug in deeply behind the toe and he then proceeded to rip the toe apart from top to bottom. Peeling apart both halves, he then tugged off each side of the toenail. And then did it all over again with the other foot. I was so dumbstruck I hardly knew how to scream and it was all over so suddenly that I could barely understand what had happened. He then bandaged up each foot, advised taking a couple of aspirins for a few days "as a precaution" and wished me a cheery "bon voyage".

A precaution? A precaution against what exactly? The stabbing pains began as soon as he had finished and continued for about a month. The precautionary aspirins did not dull the pain and neither did anything else. The only precaution was to resolve never to set foot – and indeed toe – inside a hospital ever again.

I limped out of the hospital on borrowed crutches. I could barely walk and both feet were throbbing. Not just throbbing, but dancing, jumping, twitching and cavorting with pain.

With just a few days to go before setting out on my French adventure, I was hobbling along like the love child of Quasimodo and the Wicked Witch.

Lesson preparation was not at the top of my agenda and in any case I was lulled into a false sense of security by the promise of a week long induction course in Paris. Assured that all would be revealed on this course, I made my way to Victoria station to get the train to Dover and the ferry to France.

Going down the escalator my face began twitching. This time I realised that the twitch was in my right eye and was not being caused by my fear of a maniacal doctor nor the sight of my feet moving to their own internal insistent rhythm.

The more I rubbed my eye, the worse the twitching became. I had a sense of déjà vu – except that I couldn't have "vu" anything out of my right eye. It was slowly closing and it reminded me of a time when I was younger when we visited my uncle's farm. I had had a similar experience then and was told that the condition had something to do with pigs. Being an inquisitive youth, I asked what could the connection be between a twitchy eye and a pig?

"Well," said Uncle Arthur, "it's not so much about the pig as about where the pig lives. A sty. You've got a stye in your eye."

And that same sensation came back to me now and I realised that I now had a stye on my right eye. Resisting the temptation to find the nearest casualty unit at a local hospital to have it treated (fearing that they would simply wrench off the offending eyelid and probably the other one as well for good measure), I decided the best thing to do would be to carry on my journey and hopefully try and sort it out on the ferry. What on earth was I thinking? How would a fairly small bar or snack shop have anything to treat a stye with?

So I limped down the escalator, squinting all the way.

What does Shakespeare have to say about troubles coming in threes? Nothing. He wasn't talking about troubles. Or threes. But you get the point. Deciding to have one last meal in England before heading for France, I found a kiosk on the station platform and bought a ham and tomato sandwich. Standing awkwardly, shifting weight from one leg to the other to maintain balance and to try and relieve the pain of my throbbing toes, and unable to focus fully on the sandwich, I took a bite out of the British Rail ham and tomato offering. What I didn't realise was that it came with one extra ingredient – a wasp.

A wasp sting on the tongue is not recommended for any occasion, but particularly not when going abroad in order to communicate in a foreign language. And especially not when hobbling along like someone auditioning for Long John Silver – a particularly apt comparison as I would soon be needing a black patch over my right eye.

I was not allergic to wasp stings. I was not allergic to nettles. I was not allergic to anything. I – like most people – just happen not to like them. They are painful. They make your tongue swell up. They are the tongue equivalent of an ingrowing toenail. Not that you could have an ingrowing tongue. Once again the secateur-wielding doctor was conjured up in my mind's eye (the others being half-closed and swollen) and I could visualise him ripping out my tongue and saying nonchalantly: "shall we rip out the tonsils for good measure as well?"

Later, many years later, I found this comment in an American medical magazine:

"It must be remembered that this all (ie the wasp sting – Ed.) happens at considerable speed and therefore the amazing design behind the event of a wasp or bee sting, however unpleasant the consequences, is only something that can fill one with awe!"

Well I know about wasps. And I know about awe. But I never thought that I would ever see them in the same sentence.

Not filled with awe, I continued on my journey into the unknown with renewed terror about the next affliction that was awaiting my body.

My fellow Central Bureau assistants milling around the station concourse did not quite know what to make of this hobbling, rasping, one-eyed and decidedly ill-humoured companion whose only reply to any polite enquiry was "nnurrrgh ththruugh uurgh". And that was English.

I can only recall with any certainty three things from that Parisian induction course.

First – that I have an immense and lifelong affinity with the Hunchback of Notre Dame.

Second – that I do not understand the evolutionary purpose of wasps.

Third – that we were told on our first day of trainee assistantship that it was highly likely that one of us would die during our year abroad. All eyes immediately turned to me and I felt a collective death wish. In unison they wished that I would die there and then and save the rest of them any anxiety for the remaining year.

I did not oblige but limped off with lolling tongue and nervous blink towards Brittany and my first lesson.

How I managed to get to Brittany without the services of an air ambulance I do not recall.

Armed with a battery of posters and postcards and newspaper cuttings and information about the monarchy and parliament and the entente cordiale and an ever so amusing tea towel explaining cricket to foreigners ("when he's out another is in until he is out and then another comes in until the end of time or at least until it rains") I prepared to meet some real French teenagers who would be eager to learn English from a real English person.

Quite whether the one-eyed, swollen-tongued, shambling bundle of nerves who fell into their classroom was the answer to all their prayers remains an open question; suffice it to say that I was not the first *assistant d'anglais* to roll up at this establishment.

It is a truth universally acknowledged that when taking up a new job it is essential to follow a failure. Preferably a squinting, gibbering, hobbling idiot who cannot even order a cup of coffee. I was so glad that I was able to fulfil that role for my successor and hope that the bastard is grateful to me. If you are the Central Bureau assistant who had such a fantastic time in Southern Brittany in the early 1970s, then you owe me big time. I, of course, had to follow Tony. Not that he spelled his name like that. Oh no, this Tony was a Toni. Toni had a car. Not only a car but a mini. Toni gave lifts to people. Toni was fantastically theatrical and put on a play for the whole school. Toni's lessons were inspirational. He made English so exciting and interesting and played Beatles songs. Toni was so funny that merely to be in his presence was to experience the essence of Monty Python. Toni knew the dead parrot sketch. In French. (And probably Norwegian too). Toni was so musical that Johnny Hallyday had allegedly asked him for advice. Toni was bilingual with a French mother.

I never met Toni. I have loathed him all my life.

I had no car. I thought myself funny and could remember extracts from The Navy Lark and the Goons, but realised too late that they were so passé as to be positively last century. I had no Beatles songs. I realised that my collection from The New Seekers and Cliff's Greatest Hits was not quite what post May 1968 France was gagging for. I was not only not bilingual but even found being monolingual a challenge.

And then came the first lesson: a group of fifteen year olds eager and willing to speak English. With all my artefacts under my arm, I staggered into the classroom to find the pupils already there and waiting with that wonderfully indefinable Gallic insouciance and hint of menace.

I am not sure what they thought of this grinning maniac (the ointment I had put on the wasp sting kept my mouth in a fixed grimace that would have served me well if auditioning for Jack the Ripper). The maniac could only shuffle along on his heels (the toes still throbbing several weeks after the NHS torture treatment). My right eye was permanently closed and my left eye was beginning to come out in sympathy. And so I looked out to them with an expectation of sympathy and an acknowledgement of human suffering.

All I got was silence and an insolent stare from about twenty teenagers.

Forgetting all the advice I had received between the dire warnings about the putative short life span of English language assistants and lectures on the monarchy, I made the fateful first mistake of many teachers who have gone before and since. I asked a question. And not just any question. A stupid question.

"What would you like to talk about today?"

Only the faintest flicker of a smile flashed across the face of my teenage tormentor before she replied with an innocence that belied her years:

"Why is oral sex more fun for lesbians?"

Chapter 2

Vorsprung durch Cricket

"Sir, what's the German for silly mid-off?" asked Jimmy.

This question usually came around 2.10pm on a Friday afternoon when the Third Form had had enough of gaining intercultural competence by evaluating the relative merits of pastimes of British and German teenagers.

Pastimes. Now that very word encapsulated much of the problem with teaching foreign languages. Teenagers did not have pastimes. Nor hobbies. Nor leisure pursuits. Nor any of the mildly patronising assumptions of the exam boards, education departments, curriculum agencies and textbook publishers. (And for that matter why were they called textbooks when most of the pages were covered in varying forms of foreign graffiti, a variety of balloons or flags, a rabid animal of some sort mouthing greetings in a manic way, a picture of a cheery sausage or witless frog, but certainly no text to speak of).

Teenagers just did things. Or they didn't. There wasn't much rhyme or reason to it. They hung about together. They went out drinking. They engaged in any number of activities. But they had neither pastimes nor hobbies. Such words conjured up bygone days of stamp collecting and skipping, camping and tying knots. Can hanging around be a hobby or poker a pastime?

Jimmy had asked this question for a number of deep psychological reasons, most of which he was blissfully unaware of. Like many boys, he attributed his failure in German to an innate lack of ability and therefore saw no purpose in making any effort to understand what was going on. Any effort would only result in further failure that would reinforce his feelings of inadequacy and rejection. As soon as I got to "Guten.." Jimmy was lost and for the rest of the lesson I might have well been speaking Swahili for all the good it did. As it happened, I was not unaware of his plight and had tried as best I could through mime and gesture to communicate the overall gist of the lesson.

I say: "also (sweeping hand gestures), heute (point to calendar) werden wir (point to next week's calendar to indicate futurity of action) lernen (open book, furrow brow then look in wonderment as the Eureka experience takes place), wie man (ignore these two words and hope for the best) in Westdeutschland (point to map of West Germany) eine Fahrkarte (dig out bus ticket) kauft (indicate by dual role-taking the offer of and acceptance of the exchange of goods by means of monetary payment)." This one sentence has taken 2 minutes and 37 seconds to perform and I am exhausted. The pupils look variously bemused, bored and bewildered.

Most pupils have heard and seen: "alzoo" (teacher looks mad) oitar (teacher trying to find date of the end of term) dooody dooda (teacher trying to find date when he can retire on full pension) mumble mumble (teacher lifts book as though about to strike someone and then thinks better of it) wie man (how one) in Westdoitschland (points to map of Uruguay) a fart (smelly piece of paper) **!?&* (teacher waving and gesticulating madly handing money to himself).

Jimmy heard and saw: mumblegrrmumble splurge kraft glurp grrr (looking out of the window at the netball team). At this point he reasoned sensibly that another forty minutes of this would be too much for either teacher or pupils to bear.

"Sir, what's the German for silly mid-off?" all wide-eyed and innocent.

Now I was an experienced teacher. I knew this sort of thing cropped up most Friday afternoons and I knew how to deflect it. Normally, I would turn the question around, engage the pupil in semantic riddles, point the class towards a higher ethic and manage both to divert the pupil from further interruption and maintain the flow of the lesson.

As Ofsted inspectors were to report about fifteen years later, the pace of a lesson was the quintessence of excellent teaching. If you had pace you got *outstanding*. If you had no pace you barely got *satisfactory*. The only trouble was that no one had ever successfully defined just what exactly "pace" meant. Shoot off like an express train and you are in danger of leaving the class behind. Build up steadily and you risk boring them to sleep. It seemed to boil down quite simply to: greet them appropriately in German and maintain total vigilance. Begin with a brisk starter activity, engaging all in an intellectually challenging task involving little stress whilst differentiating the activity so as to include all pupils equally; then moving seamlessly to the core of the lesson outlining all learning objectives and pupil target language outcomes with sufficient modelling and indication of necessary resources, allocate groups of mixed ability maintaining gender balance (and keeping Jimmy away from Wayne); provide enough stimulus to engage the pupils' attention and then through judicious interventions and timely questions keep the lesson on track. Ensure that all questions are stretching, open, ethical, balanced, rigorous, robust, pithy, thoughtful and requiring a carefully considered response.

Jimmy's question seemed to me to fit all the criteria so I allowed myself some wait time to think up a response. It really was amazing how many thoughts could flash through your mind in nanoseconds once the synapses in the brain got working and made the appropriate connections.

German. Cricket.

In no time at all I was transported back five years to a field of clover and daisies and dandelions in the north of West Germany where I had attempted the unlikely task of teaching a group of German pupils how to play cricket. It was during my stint as a teacher during the 1970s in a highly respected *Gymnasium* (or grammar school) in a small town in West Germany that I had tried to explain to a group of fifteen year olds just what exactly cricket was. My explanations had failed dismally and I reasoned that the only way they could fully appreciate the game would be to teach them.

Which explanation is easier to grasp:

Law 29.1 makes it quite clear what conditions are to be satisfied for a batsman to be considered within his ground or, in the phrase of Law 18, to have **'made good his ground'**. Whenever the wicket is put down at his end, each umpire must know whether or not the batsman was in his ground. If the batsmen run, each umpire must check, for every run attempted, that it is not a short run. He must see the batsman complete it by grounding (occasionally) some part of his person or (usually) his bat behind the **popping crease** at his end. The batsman's hand must be in contact with the bat at the time. The **striker's end** umpire is in a good position to do this, being square on to the creases. Sometimes he will have to move a little to one side to avoid being unsighted by a fielder. The umpire at the bowler's end has to move to a position **square with the creases** as quickly as he can after the ball is played. Usually this will be to the side to which the ball has been played. When a batsman has a **runner**, it will have to be to the side opposite to the one where the runner is. This is for the umpire to avoid the risk that the runner might be behind him.

Taken from the 151 page manual MCC Laws of Cricket (2000 Code 3rd Edition – 2008).

Or

To form the past participle of **weak verbs**, you add *ge-* to the beginning of the verb stem and *–t* to the end.
To form the past participle of **strong verbs**, you add *ge-* to the beginning of the verb stem and *–en* to the end. The vowel in the stem may also change.
To form the past participle of **mixed verbs**, you add *ge-* to the beginning of the verb stem, and like weak verbs, -*t* to the end. As with many strong verbs, the stem vowel may also change.

Taken from Collins Easy Learning German Grammar (2005).

The problem with both texts is that they are immediately clear and obvious to an *aficionado* of either cricket or German but to an outsider, un étranger, ein Fremder or simply someone who has no interest in either subject, they are baffling. The bafflement comes both from the language used and the content being communicated.

How long would it take me to explain all of these technical words or phrases before you understood the texts above?

Made good his ground
Short run
Popping crease
The striker's end
Square with the creases
A runner

And even then I am making the assumption that batsman / umpire / wicket / run are generally understood.

The same applies with the text on German grammar:

Weak verb
Strong verb
Mixed verb
Past participle
Stem

And are the words vowel and verb also generally understood?

Even when the individual words have been explained and clarified at great length, would the communication be any clearer?

"so, let me get this clear: if the batsman, the person holding the bat (wooden object for the purpose of striking the ball), who is attempting to score runs (points) by hitting the ball (spherical object – usually red) and running up and down the pitch (ground), steps over the popping crease (line drawn parallel with the wicket (three stumps ([long stick]) in the ground – not to be confused with the bowling crease) after completing his run (point) before the said wicket is broken (knocked over by ball thrown by fielder) (one of the opposing side), then he can be said to have "made his ground" and remains "in" (ie not out – still able to remain and score runs (points)) and not "out" (ie has to leave the field of play)."

It is only after the context, action and rationale have fully been grasped that the explanation would make any sense at all. And that would probably come by osmosis through a long period of watching, absorbing, listening and actively being engaged in the activity itself. Being born into a cricket family also helps.

The same may be said to apply to German grammar.

"A strong verb is in essence an irregular (ie does not conform to the usual pattern) verb (doing word – see chapter 7) formation whereas a weak verb is a regular verb that does conform to the usual pattern of verb formation".

A mixed verb is just taking the piss.

Therefore, we can only draw one conclusion from this: only explain when they already understand.

German grammar certainly became clearer to me after spending a significant amount of time in Germany. No amount of explanation could have made up for the listening, absorbing and experiencing the nuances of German speech and writing. After all of that, the strong and weak and mixed verbs more or less fell into place.

Much the same could be said of trying to talk about cricket to German teenagers. This was a fairly pointless exercise until they had experienced the game for themselves and could then appropriate the laws with aplomb.

To my surprise they simply loved the game, and although some of the finer points were lost on them (just how do you explain the logic of no more than two people fielding behind the batsman on the legside? Even Hegel would have struggled with that), they managed to pick up the rudiments fairly quickly.

The girls were as enthusiastic as the boys and provided they only played with tennis balls and used rounders bats, then they were on pretty safe ground. Many happy hours were spent playing a game that resembled something between rounders, softball, netball and the United Nations Security Council.

"No, Heidi, you cannot run around the ground when you hit the ball. *Das ist verboten.* No, Dieter, you are not allowed to throw the ball at the batsman's head. *Das ist verboten.* No, Karl, you are not allowed to use a stump instead of a bat if you dropped it during the last run. *Das ist verboten.*"

In fact almost everything they tried to do was *verboten,* but they didn't mind that so much because that was true of school and home life anyway.

At that time in West Germany it was *verboten:*

- to beat carpets in the afternoon between noon and 3pm
- to go shopping after 5pm on weekdays and after 1pm on a Saturday
- to take round to a friend's house an even number of flowers
- not to take flowers to a cemetery on a Sunday
- to be late for anything under any circumstances
- not to eat at least one slice each of several enormous cakes when invited to Frau Meinert's for Kaffee und Kuchen
- to call anyone anything other than Herr Doktor Doktor Professor Schuldirektor until you had sworn undying faithfulness and brotherly love, entwined arms and drunk several pints of cold beer together
- not to accept that the third goal in 1966 was dubious when looked at from the camera angle of a *Stern* reporter's grainy photo

- to suggest that a teacher had a cushy life after two lessons in the morning and packing up at 1pm every day
- to cross the road anywhere where there was not a little green man.

You were allowed to mention the war.

In fact, teaching cricket to the Germans and ruminating on the war were brought together one day when my team of motley teenagers were challenged to a match by the local British Army school. Somehow news of these strange goings-on at the local school had been drawn to the attention of Her Majesty's Forces stationed in the town's garrison. The town had a population of about 70,000. The British Army had stationed several thousand troops there. Because they were a mere 25 km from the Iron Curtain they had been given clear orders in the event of attack from the East: hold the town for 24 hours and then get the hell out of there.

There was a school on the camp catering for the children of the army personnel. And they had a cricket pitch and real equipment. When I received the invitation for a match, I was not sure how my fledging German cricketers would react. They were only used to gentle matches involving tennis balls, fields of daisies and plenty of dubious ways of getting out as well as staying in even though plumb LBW because the umpire had no idea about the laws of cricket.

However, upon receiving the invitation, they were wildly enthusiastic. They now saw a chance to avenge 1966 in their own way, see the inside of the mysterious garrison and practise their *Gymnasium* English on the unsuspecting sons and daughters of the British Army. I had at least been able to wring one concession out of my army counterpart – this would be a mixed team with at least four girls per team.

Now I was no mug. I knew that my team faced annihilation and so tried to prepare them for the fixture with giving not only extra practice sessions but also some insights into English psychology when it came to sport. The first thing I did was to try to find some real cricket balls. With the fixture only a fortnight away I didn't want my team to face real cricket balls for the first time on an uneven pitch beyond the ceremonial parade-ground. I knew that I had no chance of finding cricket balls in the sports shops in Celle and so I contacted a sports firm in England and ordered six balls to be shipped out as soon as possible.

This of course was in the mid 1970s when not only were Baader-Meinhof turning West German society upside down with their terror attacks but the IRA were also attacking British Army bases on the Continent. So when a suspicious package of six spherical red objects arrived at the *Zollamt*, Celle's Customs' Office, I was immediately summoned to meet the head customs officer, Herr Dietmeyer.

I understood his predicament but also saw that it was well nigh impossible to explain to a German customs officer what a cricket ball was when they had no concept of the sport. If there was no concept there was no word, as someone definitely memorable but instantly forgettable had once pronounced.

I had to admit that to an outsider they did look suspiciously like grenades – red, round, heavy, a distinctive rim and no possible earthly use for any legal activity ever invented or conceived of in West Germany.

"So", Herr Grin "perheps you vould like to explain just von more time vot zese spherical objects are."
"Balls," was of course the facetious reply, but I knew that semantic humour was not likely to get me out of this predicament.   Not only would the balls be impounded but my nervous team would have no idea what was about to hit them (almost certainly literally).

"Well," I began dubiously, "we are having a cricket match against the British army school in town and I wanted to introduce my pupils to the real equipment that we use in England."

"Hm, cricket," said Herr Dietmeyer, "und so how is zet played again? It is like baseball, ja, only very slow und dull. I hav heard zet some metches can go on for as much as zree hours. Zis must be very boring indeed for zee spectators. Is it true zet all zee players are also vearing vite?"

I did not have the heart to tell him about three day county matches or even five day test matches, but realised that I would have to humour him if I was to have any chance of getting hold of the cricket balls at all.

"Well, Herr Dietmeyer, cricket is a complex game with complex rules, but the basic idea is quite simple. The object of the game is to win more points than the opposition. Each team scores points by hitting a cricket ball (I thought I had better mention these as often as possible so that I might have a chance of getting out with what I had come for) as far as they can and then running up and down before the other team can get the ball back to the middle. They hit the ball with a bat and there are two players with bats at any one time. They run up and down whilst the opposition are trying to get the ball back to the middle so they can bowl it again...." (at this point I noticed a glazing over the eyes, a fixed quizzical look and a somewhat constipated expression that I would later in life come to be very familiar with whenever I tried to explain the pluperfect to GCSE classes). I paused. I detected no sign of understanding at all, not a flicker or smidgeon of recognition from Herr Dietmeyer and so I stopped altogether. It was then that I had my Eureka moment. Instead of trying to explain the inexplicable, I would simply give Herr Dietmeyer the opportunity of discovering the joys of cricket for himself.

"Look," I continued, "I think it will take quite a long time for me to explain all there is to know about the game of cricket. Would you like to come and see our match against the British Army school and then you could see for yourself how it is played and how much enjoyment the pupils are getting from the experience? We are due to play in a couple of weeks time and we are hoping for a good crowd to encourage the home team."

"Vell," said Herr Dietmeyer, "zet sounds en excellent idea. Just give me zee time und location und I vill come along and support zee school team. Und I suppose you hed better heff zese cricket balls to prectise viz. Ve vould not vant zee army school to haf all zee advantages."

I could not believe my luck. Not only would I get the balls to practise with, but I might even get a crowd (well one or two parents) as well. It was just as I was about to leave the customs' office when Herr Dietmeyer brought home to me the Realpolitik of working in a *Gymnasium* at that time. There were three compulsory subjects that were essential for pupils to do well in if they wished to progress to the next year and not be kept down for a year. The dreaded *"sitzenbleiben"* (literally "stay sitting") hung over the heads of all German schoolchildren and parents would do all they could to ensure that their children did not suffer the extra year's schooling that a bad mark would require them to have. The subjects were German, maths and English. Because the class tests were internally set and marked, this gave enormous power to teachers because one or two bad marks in those crucial subjects could seriously handicap a pupil's progress through school.

"Meine Tochter, Erika, says zet she really likes English und you are her favourite teacher." I racked my brains. Of course, Erika Dietmeyer. That quiet little girl who sat in the corner and said very little to me or anyone else. Her marks had been uniformly bad all year and one more poor test could send her into the relegation zone. She was also on the fringes of selection for the cricket team – mainly because of her ability to take catches near the wicket. The next test was due in about three weeks time, just after the cricket match.

Not that Herr Dietmeyer's relaxation in the regulations about cricket balls could in any way be construed as bribery or corruption.

"I do hope zet she vill do vell in her next English test; it vould be such a shame if she vere to do bedly. I em sure zet if zee cricket game vent ahead, zis would give her just zee confidence she needs, ja?

Well, that and the whole of English grammar, the vagaries of spelling, the subtleties of syntax, use of irony and a modicum of knowledge of vocabulary. But I sensed victory and so grasped the opportunity.

"Many thanks," Herr Dietmeyer. "I am also sure that a good game of cricket is all she needs. If she can understand half of what the game is about, the rest of English syntax should be a piece of cake."

The summer of 1975. Hot. Languid. Not a drop of rain for months.

The first priority was to find the right equipment for the team. We had the nice shiny new cricket balls, courtesy of the friendly *Zollamtmeister,* and I had managed to borrow some bats and pads from a local team. I presumed that the army would be able to provide the rest of the equipment. However, we had no cricket whites and I was determined that we would appear as competent and orthodox as possible to give the army team a run for its money.

White trousers were a non-starter. There was no echelon of West German society that wore white trousers. We compromised with white shorts (used in the playing of Handball), white socks (ditto) and white T-shirts (ditto – and a useful distraction when worn by the girls).

The game was brief and inglorious and can be best summed up by the team scoresheet which records for posterity our first and last away fixture as Hölty-Gymnasium First XI.

Hölty-Gymnasium : First (and only) Innings

	Batsman	How Out	Bowler	Runs
1	Petra	Ran away because ball too hard	Smith	0
2	Michael	Ran after Petra	Smith	0
3	Suzanne	Preferred making a daisy chain	Smith	0
4	Dieter	Shouting	Smith	0

5	Stefan	Hit wicket and wicketkeeper	Smith	0
6	Detlev	Refused to take guard	Smith	0
7	Armgard	Forgot to bring bat	Smith	0
8	Bernd	Caught ball instead of hitting it	Smith	0
9	Christoph	Tried to head the ball	Smith	0
10	Erika	LKW [1] (German joke: untranslatable)	Smith	0
11	Franz	Went off for a burger (and carried ball over boundary)	Smith	4
Extras				0
			Total	4

Smith: 2 – 0 – 4 - 10

Needless to say, the army school knocked off the runs in less than one over.

Franz: 0.1 – 0 – 6 - 0

We declined the offer of a beer match and set off home to lick our wounds.

"So now I understand it," said Herr Dietmeyer with a big smile on his face. "Zis half of zee field is playing against zee ozer half. Zee one viz zee big stick is trying to make zee uzzer von viz zee big stick – how you say – get outed. Zis much is clear. But how do you know who zee opposition is if zey are all vearing vite?"

---

[1] LKW *Lastkraftwagen* (lorry) – LBW Leg before wicket – well that's German humour for you

Chapter 3

Irritable vowel syndrome

"A teacher can no more deliver a lesson than a postman teach a letter"

What is a lesson? Who decided that a lesson would constitute forty-five minutes of instruction from a teacher and a similar amount of time of passive absorption from pupils? Who then decreed that six doses of this regime on a daily basis over many years would constitute an education? Did the faceless ones who made such an arrangement realise that on any given day, up and down the country, teachers would be teaching and pupils would be learning.

Except that teachers would be teaching one thing and pupils learning another. Teachers often focused on the content of what they had to teach and tried to arrange it in as palatable form as was humanly possible so that pupils would learn in the same way.

Modern languages teachers often presented material, rehearsed it with the class and then expected some performance of that material in written or spoken form. By setting out a series of vocabulary items in an attractive fashion and by inviting pupils to repeat, it was generally felt that pupils would absorb the relevant material more or less satisfactorily.

Pupils often learnt other lessons. During forty-five minutes they could learn how to appear interested in ten French colours whilst all of the time working out their next move in *Death Strike 3*. They could very quickly learn that with certain teachers making animal noises and loud bodily functions would soon leave a lesson in tatters. An overhead projector could be sabotaged with a few deft knocks from a desk, cassette players could easily be rewound thus leaving the teacher in a state of apoplexy when announcing the next listening exercise, in fact anything technological could be derailed for one simple reason: the pupils always knew more about the technology than the teacher. Therefore they could keep one step ahead and lead the teacher a merry dance whilst all the time feigning real interest.

"Honest, Miss, if you press Ctrl+Alt+Del, the PC will automatically display all the files you want."

Hadn't those who designed technological devices ever seen the speed with which children in the early 1980s could solve a Rubik's cube puzzle in a matter of seconds, whilst adults took hours? And ten years after that Game Boys were all the rage with under sevens whilst well-meaning parents looked on in nervous apprehension. Only ten years further on and pupils could text each other messages, record thousands of tunes on iPods, take photos on mobile phones, check their email and download internet images on those same phones, calculate all manner of football scores and likely implications of separate results, know the top forty in any pop chart on any given day, understand all the complex interrelationships in a dozen different soaps … and yet not be able to learn ten simple pets in French. And their gender. And yes, Lucy, spelling does count. And yes, Callum, those funny little squiggles count as spelling as well.

So the teachers, using 19th century methodology and psychology (bits of paper, idle threats, pleading, bribery, force of personality) tried to instil into their pupils (versed in 20th century technology and adept at distraction techniques) a knowledge and love of a foreign language which at best they would be able to chalk up as another Grade C in the endless and inexhaustible drive for higher standards and at worst they would regard as a futile exercise in European indoctrination.

These and other thoughts did not unduly concern me as I prepared for my second lesson of the week with Year 7. I had just dismissed Year 9 and was enjoying that two minute hiatus between lessons before the next group arrived. I had the luxury of teaching in the same room for most of the time and so I expected pupils to come to me rather than going in search of them.

This arrangement suited me admirably and meant that I often had time to prepare my materials before the next group arrived.

First I would write up my learning objectives for the class on the whiteboard. Ofsted had insisted on at least three and so I dutifully wrote on the board:

Learning Objectives for Today's Lesson:

Pupils will learn how to develop intercultural understanding and linguistic competence using word level utterances both orally and in written form

Pupils will engage in meaningful transactional dialogues with others and assess rigorously and robustly their peers

At this point I wanted to write (... *and have a bit of* fun) but realised that that would never do, and so I continued:

Pupils will perform ludic activities to show emotional intelligence and awareness of multicultural diversity and the advantages of plurilingualism.

I then checked that the cassette recorder was switched on and that the tape was in the right place. Next I found the right video and fast-forwarded it to the two minute clip I intended to use. I just had time to fetch the starter activity before the first pupil arrived at the door.

"Bonjour, Tracy. Tu veux m'aider?" I said enquiringly as a curly haired girl insinuated herself into the room clutching a lipstick, a mirror, a mascara brush and a half-eaten sandwich.

"Wot?"

At this point I made rapid judgement call and reverted to the mother tongue.

"Could you please put these handouts on each of the desks? Thanks."

"Oh, sir. 'Snot fair. Do I have to?"

"Yes, please," I said briskly, trying to sort through 110 flashcards for the appropriate 10. I always promised myself that I would one day make my own flashcards, as I had been encouraged to do as a student teacher a couple of decades ago; ("it's much more authentic / culturally significant / personal, and when they are laminated they will last for a lifetime") but somehow never quite got round to it.

Flashcards. That was always a strange word and made the pupils titter and giggle. Like "gist" and "text". Pupils could find any word embarrassing, awkward, sinister and once they had discovered its secret powers there was nothing I or any other teacher could ever do to put the genie back in the bottle and use the word in all its primeval innocence.

Flashcards. Whoever dreamt that up? Must have been demented. The idea was simple enough. Use a pictorial representation of the word you are trying to convey through the foreign language to help the learner gather the meaning of the word without (and here is the heresy that dare not speak its name) having to resort to ... English. Simple enough. *Un chien*. Show picture of dog. (Wot's that, sir? Looks like a pig with a rupture). *Une maison*. Show picture of house. (Our house hasn't got four windows / a garden / a garage / a roof / any bricks / any doors etc). But then comes the real challenge – and the thing that made me give up any idea of creating my own flashcards. *Vite*. At this point commercial artists temporarily take leave of their senses and forget that they are trying to convey to childlike little souls the simple meaning of the word "quickly". They come over all post-modern and artistic and draw a demented chicken racing like a lunatic across a farmyard being followed by a snarling axe-wielding farmer.

Teacher holds up said flashcard of panic stricken poultry.

"Répétez. Vite"

Pupils: "Vite" (and thinking "**chicken crazy**")

The next shows a bull rushing maniacally around a china shop shattering everything in sight (why on earth do they use animals to describe adverbs?)

"Répétez. Soigneusement"

Pupils: "Swanoosemon" (and thinking "**china smashing**")

The third and final one in this sequence displays a Cheshire cat grinning malevolently and about to pounce on an unsuspecting little mouse:

"Répétez. Heureusement"

Pupils: "Herurrzemon" (and thinking "**psychopathic**")

So, when asked to put one or more of these newly learned words into a sentence, one pupil comes up with an offering that can roughly be translated as:

"My brother runs like a crazy chicken for the bus whilst my psychopathic sister smashes all the china in the house."

The teacher is delighted at the correct usage of three adverbs, the inspector is impressed by the pronunciation of the pupil and the pupils continue to think the French barmy and the learning of French akin to dubious psychological practices carried out by armies in defiance of the Geneva convention. Samantha, who has just uttered the immortal and phonetically correct line, is still trying to figure out how she will use such sentiments in her next correspondence to Jean-Paul, her newly discovered French *copain*.

By now all of the pupils have trooped in, sat obligingly at their desks and are staring in mild disbelief, incomprehension and some bemusement at the handout in front of them. In an attempt to give a starter that required the minimum of input from myself and the maximum of effort from the pupils, I had produced a series of seemingly random French words and I wanted the pupils to categorise them in as many different ways as possible. The laudable intention was to show the pupils the similarities in the form of the words (spelling / accents) and thus make it easier for them to remember. The words were all connected with food and drink and most of them had been met before. The starter activity had been planned to last five minutes – just long enough to engage their little minds, provide appropriate intellectual demands for the brightest and yet not deter the more intellectually challenged, and just long enough for me to settle everyone down, check the register, prepare the next activity to allow for a suitably smooth transition (Inspectors just loved smooth transitions – "Mr Green, your lesson did not exhibit enough smooth transitions" – as if it was some kind of pole dance that could slip from one position to the other without anyone noticing).

pain / chocolat / beurre / toast / confiture / café / thé / citron / oeuf / jambon / melon / pâté

What I intended and what I got were always two very loosely connected events. The intended pupil learning outcome would have been something along the lines of:

Café – thé – pâté: all end in the grapheme (é) and phoneme (é)

Citron / melon: both have the phoneme-grapheme correspondence (on)

Toast / melon / café / thé / chocolat: all cognates

This would be assessed informally: "see how recognition of cognates makes learning the spelling and meaning of French words so much easier". This would take place during the plenary session – formerly known as "giving-out-homework-whilst-packing-up-and-collecting-in-vocab-test-results-putting-away-dictionaries-seeing-Kevin-and-Callum-at-the-end-of-the-lesson session"

What I got was:

"Sir, I don't get it"
"Chocolat – isn't that that French film that was on over Christmas?"
"Jambon – jam good – so that must go with toast"
"Citron – they're crap cars. My dad says all French cars are crap. That's why we've got a Purjaut – Italian is best. Sir, what car 'av you got?"
"Well melon is a fruit. Beurre is obviously berry – so that's a fruit too. And you eat fruit in a café – so they all go together."

Intervening in facilitator mode, I decided to ask some challenging questions – not closed questions that only required yes/no response and not specific questions that only demanded recall of knowledge and would have Dr Bloom tut-tutting up his Taxonomy – these would be open ended, challenging yet attainable, thought-provoking yet requiring synthesis and analytical skill:

"Will you all shut up?" was the first, albeit rhetorical, one – this had an immediate response. The pupils ignored me.

I then thought of injecting a little humour – would it be the reference to *un chapeau melon* (a bowler hat) or my all time favourite:

"Please quieten down now. After all, *un oeuf* is enough."

Whether or not the pupils understood the homophonic pun, it had the desired effect and after the statutory five minute starter, I was ready to start the Lesson Proper.

It all seemed so much easier twenty years ago. There were no intended learning objectives and pupil learning outcomes. There was certainly less technology, less paperwork and no inspectors breathing down your neck. Lesson preparation for the First Form consisted of choosing which ten or so words (usually nouns) you were going to concentrate on in that lesson. You would then think up a couple of activities to play around with those words. Explanations of any connections to preceding lessons were certainly done in English and the whole lesson was rounded off with a game of hangman. Homework was learning the ten words and a vocab test would start off the next lesson. Anyone with less than ten out of ten would have to copy out all the unlearnt words three times and then the whole cycle would begin all over again.

Written work consisted of "Copying from the board", "Drawing and labelling" (always a firm favourite with the girls), "Wordsearches", "Crosswords" and if you felt really avant-garde "Gap fill".

By the end of the term pupils would have come into contact with about a hundred French words. By the end of the year about three hundred. By the start of the following year, The Second Form, they would have forgotten 95% of the words and so the whole process would begin all over again. I remembered teaching the same set of words and phrases to successive lessons of First Form, Second Form, Third Form, Fourth Form and Fifth Form. They then took O level and came out with grade U. It didn't make for inspiring teaching. But it did make lesson preparation a lot easier.

"Right," I said. "Who can tell me today's lesson objectives?" and pointed at the board. A hand went up.

"Yes, Samantha."

"We are going to mangle action logs and assess our busts."

At the sound of the word "busts" Wayne and Jimmy stopped trying to make soggy paper stick to the ceiling by surreptitiously spitting.

"Phwoar! Whose boobs are we going to start with?"

Before the whole lesson went to pieces I quickly stepped in.

"Right, that's enough."

"Do you mean un oeuf?" said Paul nonchalantly.

"Moving on, we are going to use the food and drink from the starter activity and learn how to buy such items in a French shop. We shall also describe the items using ten new colours which we shall learn today." (When all's said and done, I thought, it always comes down to ten new words.)

Eschewing flashcards, I decided to introduce the colours by simply writing the French word on the board, asking the pupils if they could see any connection to an English word and hopefully by the end of the lesson they would have established firm links between the French colours and the English ones. There was no Ofsted inspector present and so no need for an insufferable amount of spoken French. The lesson had picked up from its doubtful start and the pupils seemed reasonably biddable.

I thought I would start with a nice easy one to get them going.

"*Bleu*"

"Why don't the French spell blue properly, sir?" piped up Hassan.

I thought back to my lectures on phonetics and linguistics as an undergraduate. I had particularly enjoyed psycholinguistics with all its idiosyncratic reasons why certain words shifted in meaning and spelling and I remembered with fondness my gentle tutor who would engage her students with delectable studies about the Chanson de Rolland. But not once had it ever occurred to me to enquire of Dr Rosemary Trevelyan why the French couldn't spell properly. This was obviously a lack in my education and would explain my inability to give a convincing answer to Hassan.

"Let's move on. *Bleu* – blue. See if you can see a connection between the next colour and an English word which also has something to do with food: *blanc*"

"Laurent Blanc. He's rubbish. He also cheats and dives all the time," said Ryan, getting animated for the first time in a French lesson in recorded history.

"No he's not. He's ace. Better than Lineker. He's just all ears and one big boot", said Dave, sensing a good argument brewing.

"This is not about football," I interjected somewhat desperately. "Can any one see any connection with food?"

"Blonk. Blonk. I don't get it, sir."

"How about if we add the word for eat – mange – then we get blancmange. Now do you see it?" I said, cutting to the chase and thinking that if they didn't hurry up they would not reach the end of the lesson at all.

"Oh, now I get it sir," said Dave. "Blonkmonje – so blonk means red."

Now this is where a sufferer from IVS (Irritable Vowel Syndrome) would empathise with my predicament. Quite how I extracted myself from that one I would never know. The smooth transition from blonk meaning red to *blanc* (notice how we don't pronounce the c) meaning white was something of which the casuists of old would have been proud. Moving swiftly on, I dealt in turn with:

noir (Northern Irish for 'now' spotted by Patrick)
gris (grizzly bear / gristle / Grease / and of course Jimmy Greaves)
rouge (rugby / rounders / rug*)*

Warming to my task, and with two of the more interesting words left to go, I felt I was finally communicating the idea of links between French and

English. I had managed to clear the dead wood surrounding *bleu / blanc / gris / noir / rouge* and I decided to cut my losses and drop *marron* and *violet*. That just left two and I felt I could cover those in the remaining five minutes and still leave time for a plenary.

"Now the next colour has something to do with a disease. It is *jaune*."

More hands went up than ever before and I felt I was at last getting through. Maybe the spelling links were paying off at last, maybe the steady drip of pronunciation, explanation, linking and repetition were coming to fruition.

"Sir, sir. Measles," said Jimmy, with a defiant confidence.
"No, sir it's got to be mumps."
"Chicken pox, sir" joined in another.
"Flu," said John.
"Scarlet fever," said Tom.

"Now hold it right there," I said. "Where on earth are you getting all these diseases from?"

"We've just done 'em in history, sir," said Henry helpfully.

"But what on earth has it got to do with *jaune*, with French?" I said in exasperation.

"Well we've just finished the French Revolution and now we are going on to Diseases of Nineteenth Century Europe."

I sighed a deep sigh. I had read many books on learning theory in my time. I had attended many learned lectures. I had even written essays a long time ago about motivation, memorisation, relevance. I had discussed the psychology of learning, the sociology of learning, the epistemology of learning, in fact all the –ologies I could think of about learning. But nothing could ever explain the extraordinary leaps of imagination and fantasy that young minds could manage without a blush of embarrassment or scintilla of shame. If I said "chien" they would immediately respond unthinkingly "Chinese" "Ice-cream Van" "Revolver" – there would be no logic or learning theory on earth that could explain how it was that a child's wandering mind could collide with a word or phrase that would set off limitless associations that would exercise Freudian and Jungian psychoanalysts for decades in trying to unravel the mysteries of collocation.

Gently, like a kindly uncle about to let a suspecting nephew know the reality about Santa Claus, I pointed out, ever so softly, almost in a whisper:

"*Jaune*. Think of the English word jaundice. Yellow fever. *Jaune* means yellow."

Stunned silence.

"Well, why didn't you say so straightaway, sir?" And I was beginning to think that myself.

"Right, we've just got one more to go. The word is *vert*. Can anyone see a connection or another English word like it?"

This time, quick as a flash, little Caitlin O'Connor's hand goes up. At last, I thought. Someone has been paying attention.

"Yes, Caitlin. And what word in English do we get from *vert*?"

Expecting anything from "Coal bucket" to "Heat seeking missile" to "French fries", I awaited the answer on tenterhooks.

"Verdant."

"Very good, Caitlin", scarcely believing my ears. The rest of the class also looked on appreciatively.

"And can you give me a phrase using verdant to show its meaning?"

"The Verdant Mary!" said Caitlin triumphantly.

Chapter 4

The speaking test: only correct

Why is it that those who are educated never learn?

The teaching of modern foreign languages has been bedevilled from the very moment when the subject itself was invented. When pupils had to learn Latin or French or German, it was fairly clear from the outset what the transaction was.

1.   Teacher knows lots of French.
2.   Pupil knows no French.
3.   Teacher teaches French.
4.   Pupil learns it.
5.   Teacher sets test.
6.   Pupil takes and fails test.
7.   Repeat from (3) ad infinitum.

Then one day, French was considered just too obvious a concept, too clear, too neat. A post-modern wave swept across education and a single subject morphed into a three-worded tangle of misconceptions, a veritable trinity of confusion: modern foreign languages. Worse was to follow when those three unremarkable words were squashed into the deadly acronym MFL.

Names are important. They have power and meaning. French means what it says. It means lots of French words and sounds and phrases and verbs and tenses and wine and cheese and sexy shrugs and the Eiffel Tower and the Arc de Triomphe. MFL sounds like a dreary store for do-it-yourself, a dodgy energy supplier or a hideous disease caught whilst engaging in a decidedly peculiar activity. It does not sound romantic, dreamy or exciting. MFL does not have the cachet of chemistry, the sexiness of psychology or even the chutzpah of PE. It is simply not cool. It is therefore doomed.

It all seemed so simple at the time and the intentions were certainly laudable.

Whilst invigilating an exam in the sports hall one day, I began to daydream about how this had all come about and thoughts returned to my own grammar school form of education. Allowed, indeed encouraged, to drop mindless pursuits such as science at a very early age (my school report simply said "Not really a scientist" and so that was that) I concentrated during my impressionable teens on French, German and Latin. What would now be regarded as scandalously lopsided and unbalanced was taken for granted in the Sixties. Half a timetable devoted to three foreign languages (one dead and two showing signs of distinct decrepitude), plenty of English grammar (parsing, clause analysis and parts of speech the order of the day), a dash of literature (Shakespeare and Orwell – of course – and Gerald Durrell's bloody family of animals which took almost a year to read – slowly, painfully, one sentence at a time read out loud by each pupil in turn). There was a nod towards

Mathematics, but endless algebra, trigonometry and geometry knocked the stuffing out of me.

"Green, let me explain this just one more time."

"Yes, sir" (Oh, please God not another explanation. The first sentence usually had me groping for something tangible to keep my mind from wandering, the second had me screwing up my eyes and grinding my pencil into the palm of my hand like Michael Caine in *The Ipcress File* to keep me from confessing, the third lost me completely and at that point I usually lost the will to live.)

"So if x equals y and b equals a, what is the sum of the square of the angle of the cosin of the tangent of the equation, given that p is an integer of q and is there honey still for tea? (or so it sounded by the time I had got to the end of the question).

At this point, a wild stab in the dark usually elicited a rain of blows from plimsoll, textbook, ruler or cricket bat (depending on what was handiest at the time).

The only answers I received to my pleas about lack of comprehension were:

"Don't worry about that now, you won't need that until the Sixth Form, although you are too thick ever to make it there, so I wouldn't worry about it anyway." Or else:

"The theorem is quite clear: $x^n + y^n = z^n$ has no non-zero integer solutions for x, y and z when $n > 2$. So is that clear now?"

Why was it that teachers never understood that more explanation always led to more befuddlement and not less? Why did they not understand that if I didn't understand what the hell they were talking about the first time, how the bloody hell would I understand any better the second or even fifty-second time around? And it was mathematics that did for me very early on.

During a routine lesson in my First Year as a keen and clean-kneed sprog, the maths teacher, known to all as Bonehead, posed the following question:

"If one towel drying on a line in the sun takes one hour to dry, how long would three towels take to dry?"

Like a shot, and like a complete idiot, I had my hand in the air. At this stage in my life I had not read Bryce Courtenay's novel *The Power of One* (how could I have, it was written in 1989), but if I had, then I would have known the immortal line: *mediocrity is the best camouflage.* Everyone else in the class seemed to have had a premonition that someone called Bryce would write something significant in years to come and so they all sat quietly and serenely upon their hands. Not so me.

"Sir, sir, three hours" I called out in triumph. Barely had the laughter died down before Bonehead mockingly gave me two options, the two options that did for my scientific education and condemned me to a life of the study and later the teaching of MFL thereafter.

"Plimsoll or cricket bat?" And as the blows were suffered in silence (I had at least learned that lesson), the greater indignity was that no one ever bothered to point out why my answer was the wrong one. After all, even getting on for fifty years later, it still seemed perfectly logical to this mathematically stunted adult that three towels would definitely take three times longer to dry than one. Any explanation to the contrary would certainly be futile.

For too long, the only way to display any modicum of knowledge in any foreign language had been to translate the thoughts, feelings and, above all, opinions of so-called native speakers into faultless English. There had also been the requirement to reverse this trend and translate English into another continental tongue, usually with disastrous results all round.

Communication had not been the purpose of those who set exam papers under the old Ordinary Level system. Indeed, communication would have been entirely outside their remit altogether. Theirs was a more lofty purpose: to show that one could render into one tongue the precise wording of another was a sign of intellectual maturity, superior mental acuity and above all, higher breeding.

After all, lowly modern languages had evolved slowly, painfully and somewhat grudgingly from the higher arts known as Classics or Greats to the really ennobled of the realm. Ancient Greek and Latin were the pinnacles of achievement and to be able to translate not only from them but into them was the quintessence of aristocratic conduct. Latin Verse Composition was reserved only for the highest élite – the crème de la crème of the education system. T'was bliss to be alive at such a time and a well-placed ablative absolute was very heaven.

Ordinary Level gave way to the General Certificate of Secondary Education around 1987 (which sounded to many like the much maligned Certificate of Secondary Education) and the story then resembled more a pantomime than a serious attempt at educational reform. O level was Cinderella, mistreated and abused at every turn and expected to do all the dirty work. GCSE and 16+ were the two Ugly Sisters of the new reform – handing out mocking speeches to poor little Cinders and beating her with criterion referencing, modular options and coursework. No longer was intellectual rigour the order of the day – relevance, topicality, communication became the watchwords. Effective communication with the ever elusive sympathetic native speaker was the cry that went out across the land.

Now I had known many native speakers of foreign languages down the years, some more sympathetic than others. There were my German colleagues who fell over themselves with shock and awe at the first hearing of an Englishman saying "Guten Morgen!" There were other German colleagues whose sympathy I needed on more than one occasion when I misconstrued schiessen (shoot) for scheissen (shit), confused Loch (hole) for Lok (train) and got into endless debates about that third goal in 1966.

Effective communication became the mantra and the back room boffins came up with a cunningly simple formula for testing such a seemingly straightforward phenomenon. Each language is taught using four skills: listening, speaking, reading and writing. So, test the pupils against all four skills in equal proportion! Away with grammar grind and pointless translation; banish prose composition and six picture essays; cast out dictation and summarising. In their place came listening comprehension, reading comprehension, writing skills and the speaking test. What could be easier? Now all that had to be done was to test the pupils against simple criteria for equal percentages of the marks available.

Rather than focus all the criteria for assessment around the candidate's ability to transpose beautiful French prose into less than mangled English writing, the back room boffins had come up with another neat and ready-made idea.

If we really want to know how pupils can communicate in a foreign language, then we need to hear them speak. And in order to ensure fairness and standardisation across the land, we shall need to record them as they utter their wise words to ever sympathetic native speakers who are drooling with anticipation to know what colour Kylie's bedroom carpet is, what Kevin's favourite school subject is and what a wayward visitor to their town might get up to on a dank and gloomy Sunday evening in June.

Such simple logic had devastating consequences across the English schooling system for over a decade. It was rather like the first person who came up with the idea of taxing every individual rather than every building and calling it with disarming ease: the poll tax. Or the first general who thought it would be a good idea to bombard enemy trenches with a million shells and then send thousands of soldiers to walk across machine gun strafing no man's land because no one could have survived such an onslaught.

In the late 1980s my experience of trying to ascertain just how much French my pupils had learnt in order to be able to engage in effective communication was mirrored by thousands of teachers across the country.

We did not do an oral exam. We did a speaking test.

Speaking tests were designed in such a way as to make the task of the teacher as complex, unpopular and tiresome as possible. Complex because all of a sudden we had to become experts in handling technology (reel-to-reel tape recorders, microphones, extension leads, stopwatches); unpopular because we had to hold the school to ransom for a week whilst taking out whole classes of pupils for testing or preparing to be tested and thus interrupting their education in cooler, sexier and chutzpah-giving subjects and involving those colleagues in invigilating and crowd control and tiresome because the routine rarely changed.

Recording pupils meant that you needed a quiet area where microphones would not pick up school bells, fire alarms, parents' car horns, deputy heads calming small groups of pupils moving in the wrong area or other senior teachers calling distant pupils away from their fags and back into school, lawnmowers programmed to be set in motion at the very nanosecond when you pressed record and play simultaneously and uttered the immortal words: "Alors, Kevin, comment tu t'appelles ?", music lessons next door, police sirens, low flying aircraft, rugby and/or choir practice (it made no odds – often the sounds were indistinguishable bringing a tear to the eye of both music and PE staff). In this haven of tranquillity you then needed a reel-to-reel tape recorder, a stopwatch and a clock (both silent of course), a microphone (pointed directly at the candidate to pick up the slightest mumble that might indicate that effective communication had taken place). Anthropologists in the jungle hovering over minute forms of reptile-like creatures for days on end in the pouring rain and trying to record their mating calls have an easier task.

Teacher : "Quel âge as-tu, Kylie? "

Kylie: "J'ai quinze ans et mon anniversaire est le douze juin. J'adore le français. "
(Effective communication)

Teacher : "Quel âge as-tu, Kylie? "
Kylie : "Oui. er, er, um (...) er (...) non"
(Not effective communication)

Next was required a hangar or departure lounge of sorts where the assembled ranks of those about to speak gathered to prepare their final utterances in the foreign tongue. This had to be near at hand so that pupils could be summoned at regular intervals and far enough away to prevent any attempt at listening in to previous participants. So there had to be a runner between venues. And a timekeeper. And several staff to cover for lessons when the Modern Languages Department were conducting these Very Important Speaking Tests because they got you Twenty-Five Percent of the Total Mark allocation. And if each Speaking Test lasted for 6-8 minutes, and there were 250 pupils taking the test, and each had to be heard for the requisite amount of time to give them every opportunity to have their 6-8 minutes of fame with the by now excessively sympathetic native speaker, then the whole school had to grind to a halt for approximately one week during the summer term. Not to mention the second foreign language. Not to mention the same process for Advanced Level Speaking Tests. Nor the mock exams when the whole procedure had to be run through again.

But Kevin and Kylie's sacred words had to be heard, recorded and sent away for examination like some exotic specimen going for analysis at the Communicable Diseases Unit (CDU) of a prestigious university. After five years of French, lesson after lesson combining a flurry of flashcards with meaningful transactions, labelling of favourite living quarters and ubiquitous pets (don't try to write stick insect just say "j'ai un chat"), descriptions of wonderful holidays (c'est bien) with disastrous travel stories (c'est pas bien), enthusing about hobbies (c'est intéressant) and talking about school subjects (c'est pas intéressant), expressing opinions (oui) and expressing forthright counter opinions (oui, mais..), communicating in a variety of tenses and persons (j'aller, tu aller, il aller, nous aller, vous aller, ils aller), it all finally came down to a 6-8 minute distillation of all that learning, all that practice, all that communicative competence, all that coaching with the Foreign Language Assistant (usually called Frédérique and as sympathetic as they come: "soo, 'ow come zat afterr fif yearrs of Frrench, zey do not av a Frrench accent like *moi*?"), all that drilling, all that heartache to the Speaking Test.

Quite simply, it was time for teacher's revenge. Large rough-necked bullies who had barely attended a lesson without interrupting every other minute to say sotto voce (I 'ate French. It's boring. Sir, why do we 'av to learn French? It's boring) quaked at the thought of opening their mouths and having to say something, anything in French without hesitation, deviation or repetition. For 6-8 minutes. And no friends around to punch, prod, make silly faces at or just giggle.

All these thoughts went through my mind as I remembered the early days of recording the Speaking Test. A grammar school boy, trained in the art of learning a foreign language, drummed out of science for lacking any notion of practicality and not allowed into useful subjects like woodwork because of the higher calling of Latin, now had the task of setting up a reel-to-reel tape recorder that had been specifically designed to defeat all attempts at winding on smoothly, coping with a stopwatch, an alarm clock, a registration sheet with enough markings on it to resemble the Rosetta stone and directing the microphone towards and not away from the suffering subject.

I also had to play the part of a decidedly sympathetic native speaker pen friend's father, a less than sympathetic waiter, a railway station official with a Kafkaesque timetable, a friendly grocer and a customs official examining a suspicious package. And all the while I had to elicit globules of French from the quivering pupil that would help the CDU decide whether to award an A grade or recommend immediate deportation on the grounds of total communication failure.

There were only 48 candidates on this particular day in late June. An early start and a late finish, a quick coffee break and a hurried sandwich should see me home in time for cocoa. 48 pupils would be put through the treadmill of stimulus-response, or role play and conversation. I would provide the ever so helpful stimulus and the pupils would respond appropriately in the foreign language. This would lead to much hearty banter, exchange of opinion, light-hearted repartee and above all Effective Communication. Following two pieces of role play of which RADA would be proud there would follow a conversation in which the pupil would reveal their innermost thoughts, their witty personality, their charming habitats and their pets' feeding habits.

Candidate Number 1: Kevin Payne.

SG: Bonjour, Kevin.
KP: What ... have we started? Is that thing recording?
SG: (Staying in role as instructed) Moi, je suis le douanier. Monsieur, ce sont vos bagages?
KP: Eh?..
SG: Les bagages .. ce sont à vous, monsieur ?
KP: (morose silence)
SG: Est-ce que vous pouvez ouvrir cette valise, Monsieur?
KP: What's "Monsieur" – we never done that.
SG: Cette valise (mime suitcase) – ouvrir (mimes open) – vous (point at Kevin)?
KP: Oh oui. Ouvrir. Valise. (grins with great satisfaction)
SG: (warming to task) ...bien. Qu'est-ce que nous avons dans cette valise? Il y a du savon, des pantalons,

une brosse à dents, une chemise, un T-shirt, et un paquet. Ce sont tous à vous monsieur? (point at Kevin and nod)

KP: Je mappel Kevin

SG :   Alors, tu as quel âge, Kevin?

KP: Yer what?

SG: Tu as quel âââage?

Never mind "the xn + yn = zn has no non-zero integer solutions for x, y and z when n > 2", the killer question to leave the most enterprising teenager totally devoid of thought and unable to string two words together is undoubtedly:

Quelles sont les attractions touristiques ...... à Grimethorpe?

Chapter 5

Banda brothers

There were three Basils that had a profound impact upon education in the 1970s: Brush, Fawlty and Bernstein. Of the three, which had the greatest long-term effect?[2]

How much of teaching is based on guilt?

There were two fundamental contributions to the guilt that infused my teaching and both started when I trained to be a teacher in the early 1970s.

I had more or less enjoyed my own learning of French as a schoolboy and thought that I could do a decent enough job of teaching languages myself. Somewhat naively I adopted early on the "pour the information in and the pupils will regurgitate it" approach to teaching and so the first few weeks of my PGCE course were something of a revelation. Not only was I made to feel guilty about my own background, upbringing and education (about which I could have done precious little), but also the way I spoke. In the early 1970s Basil Bernstein had had a huge impact on teacher education programmes.

---

[2] Clue: neither the fox nor the hotel owner.

Bernstein more or less implied that middle-class pupils spoke in a particular way and so they benefited from an education system that rewarded this "elaborated code". Working-class children also spoke in a particular way, but because this was a "restricted code" they did not have access to learning in quite the same way and so they were doomed to failure from the outset.

Their very speech patterns betrayed their lack of linguistic skill and this permeated their writing as well and so they could not perform as well as their middle-class counterparts. Given that teachers came by and large from middle-class backgrounds and used this "elaborated code" in their instruction, then it was not surprising that working-class children rejected it. They simply did not understand what the teachers were talking about, *and it was the teachers' fault.* Now, Bernstein did not explicitly blame the teachers in this way but this was the inference that my colleagues and I picked up and we felt inadequate to repel the ideas.

How could you change your whole personality, speech patterns, vocabulary so as to communicate more effectively with those with a "restricted code" of language? It was like trying to talk about philosophical concepts to very young children or else anything to do with British culture to the French. How could you convey notions such as "keeping a stiff upper lip", "fair play", "mild for the time of year" and "getting your leg over on a Friday night" to citizens of Paris?

The other matter that was made clear to me right at the outset of my PGCE was that quite clearly, *and all the research backed this up*, I had been taught French and German totally wrongly. The grammar-translation method of my grammar school days was muddled, ineffective and inadequate for modern times. How true was it that I, having had five years up to O level, two years to A level and three years at University studying both French and German, could not even order a simple cup of coffee in a café in Paris? This fact was indisputable and with all my other colleagues I had squirmed in embarrassment when the tutor had challenged us all with this simple statistic: 95% of British languages graduates when faced with an opportunity to communicate in a foreign language feign urgent appointments with dentists, sudden palpitations requiring emergency nipping into a pharmacy or momentary amnesia "Excusez-moi...euh .. j'ai perdu mon chat..." along with deep blushing. The other 5% probably lied to the researcher.

The tutor, the redoutable JJ, had then proceeded to teach us conversational Italian using only listening and speaking. There was no writing and no reading. The group simply heard JJ's words or phrases and imitated them back to him when prompted. After four hours of intensive tuition we could hold a rudimentary conversation in Italian about finding our way around an imaginary town and ending up at the pizzeria. The proof of the pudding was in the pizza, so to speak, and the results quite startling. In just four hours we could converse more in a simple fashion in a new language than we could have spoken in the language we had studied for more than *eight years* at school and university.

These two experiences instilled into me the following inalienable facts about teaching:

- You are guilty
- You can do nothing about this and it's all your fault
- The pupils speak a different language
- They will not even understand your English let alone anything else
- All that you learned in the past was a complete waste of time
- Grammar bad
- Speaking good
- Writing bad
- Speaking good

Both Kafka and Orwell would have delighted to see how their lessons of life had come to pass.

Armed with these facts, I set forth to teach. It was as if a Crusader had been relieved of his faith, sword and lance and told to go off and find the Holy Grail. In Barnsley.

Now, of course, JJ did not simply leave me and my contemporaries wallowing in guilt and frustration. He provided me with a whole new set of guidelines and techniques for teaching French and German.

Grammar bad. Writing bad. That much was established and so all that was needed was a new way of teaching communication that relied not on these old-fashioned and warped ideas (which implicitly were only of use to those with knowledge of the "elaborated code") but on a scientifically proven method. A method which had its basis in science and laboratories and research and psychology and which had been thoroughly tested on rats without giving them much more than a mild headache. Not only was such research so compelling, so convincing it was also American and therefore by definition new and better and right. How could anyone possibly complain?

The method was simplicity itself and based on behaviourist psychology. The very mention of psychology in the 1970s was enough to convince us that this was the cutting edge of pedagogy, the very foundation of learning. Nowadays every pupil can do an -ology and anyone without at least a passing knowledge of psychosexual deviant behaviour is considered to be talking very restricted code.

Method of Teaching French Using Behaviourist Psychology - Part One

Teacher: Provide Stimulus (S) - chien

Method of Teaching French Using Behaviourist Psychology - Part Two

Pupil: Provide Response (R) - chien

Method of Teaching French Using Behaviourist Psychology - Part Three

Continue ad infinitum / ad nauseam until all vocabulary mastered. The End.

The Stimulus/Response (S/R) method did not stop merely with the teacher pronouncing words for pupils to repeat. Because this was *scientific* and *American* it also used the very latest in technology so that the whole process could be speeded up. One teacher pronouncing one word to individual pupils in turn would simply take too long. What if one teacher could speak to each individual pupil in turn *simultaneously* so that they could all respond in their own way and in their own time? Just as rocket scientists were finding a way to send man to the moon with the same amount of technology to make a toaster, so their counterparts in the education world invented a way of making pupils learn French more humanely, faster and more efficiently: the Language Laboratory! If rats could do it, why not pupils?

Now all the pupils could be tuned in simultaneously to each other and the teacher, they could follow the One True Method and learn French without pain (*sans pain*). And so it came to pass that every new comprehensive school in the 1970s had to have on display a shiny new language laboratory for parents to see on Open Day, governors to comment on in their reports and educationalists (for such there were) to write learned and scientific research articles praising their worth and indicating a future where all pupils could be plugged in, dosed up with French, unplugged and set off ordering cups of coffee to their little heart's content.

There was just one teeny weeny problem with this Utopian state of affairs:
the teachers did not know how to operate the equipment.

Oh and...

although they had a laboratory, there were no technicians.

Oh and...

they often broke down and could not be repaired.

Oh and...

the pupils liked to use the microphones for sending *Z Cars* messages to each other

Oh and..

the pupils quickly realised that chewing gum could sabotage a lesson instantly

Oh and...

there were few recordings of French or German available for teachers

Oh and...

the methodology was flawed. S/R. It may have worked on rats but it didn't work on pupils. They simply parroted meaningless words and learned a lot of babble.

Language labs quickly became very useful (and very expensive) store cupboards and the scientists looked elsewhere for their inspiration.

They found it in motion pictures. Not Disney of course. Sadly. That would have been quite good. Donald Duck talking French.

S/R was not seen to be the villain at this point. It was simply that the teachers were not doing it properly (guilt again). What they needed was a fully functioning audio-visual system to present the rat-tried-and-tested stimulus-response technique in a more interesting, dynamic and colourful manner.

And so my colleagues and I were thoroughly drilled in the secret art of AVMFL with reel-to-reel tape recorders, looped film slides, overhead projectors and screens in an heroic attempt at Mass Communication. We were expected to put all of this state-of-the-art technology to use during our first year of teaching. This was the time when we were at our most vulnerable, had little or no experience of working with children, found it difficult to remember thirty-two different names in each class and had never learnt languages this way ourselves. This first year was known as The Probationary Year. We were on probation but without the kindly support of a probation officer, the reassurance that our case would be reviewed or even tagging. It was like being a novice nun without the fun and glamour.

There were three essential rules for surviving the Probationary Year: (1) do not sit in the Head of History's chair (2) do not use anyone else's tea / coffee / spoon / milk / biscuits and (3) never, ever, for any reason whatsoever even think of admitting to the slightest problem with any class under any circumstances or any provocation. That would immediately set you apart as a Weak Teacher and you would be given all the bottom sets, the most difficult classes to cover for and bus duty on a Friday afternoon.

As a Probationary Teacher, you were fixed in a kind of limbo. Allowed to teach and yet not invested with the full authority of Qualified Teacher Status (QTS). I like the notion of status. Most people assume that status implies power, influence, respect and its symbols are smart cars, large houses and a salary to match. QTS was a different kind of status. It was more of a *status quo.* Someone somewhere had to decide if you were a fit and proper person to be allowed to teach and provided you were not going to upset the custom and practice of centuries, you were allowed to join the profession.

The period of probation lasted one year and was then decided on the whim of the head and LEA. If you fitted in, turned up for work and did not upset too many people, then you passed through to the next grade.

As a younger entrant to the profession, you were of course expected to teach in a variety of classrooms from one end of the school to another. I quickly learned that transporting the tape recorder, slide projector, set of exercise books and other paraphernalia from room to room was a recipe for disaster, and a bad back. So I planned my lessons not according to curricular constraints but on the basis of the proximity of the room to the store cupboard, the number of sockets in any given Portakabin and the weather forecast. If dry and close by, then the full AVMFL treatment. If wet, then the wonder of worksheets.

I simply don't know who invented worksheets. During my grammar school education we had an exercise book for every subject and copied most things from the blackboard. By the time I had reached my first school for my probationary year, worksheets were like confetti: small bits of coloured paper thrown around with joyous abandon, ending up in a soggy mess on the floor

Now worksheets came in three categories: commercial, Gestetner, Banda. Rather like Gold, Silver and Bronze. First, commercially produced – colourful, easy to read, in a boxed set, enough to go round, answers provided and so popular that I never saw them because other members of the department needed them more urgently.

Second, Gestetnered. It is difficult across the years to describe adequately the terrible joy of typing onto a Gestetner sheet.

Of course the first obstacle was the typewriter itself. Office staff could not possibly be expected to type Foreign Words – that was against their job description and there were dark rumours about poor Miss Smythe who had to have three weeks off after being required to type onto a Gestetner the O level French exam paper. "The acutes and graves I could just about cope with, but when it came to circumflexes I started to have palpitations. And it was them cedillas that finished me off completely. It wasn't part of my Secretarial Qualification grade 3 (100 words a minute). They were English words. Foreign slows you down and no mistake. I could only manage about 20 a minute and my nerves were shot to pieces. They should speak English anyway and stop all this mucking about."

So I had to do the typing myself. I had often used my typewriter (portable) for various domestic purposes, but it was another thing altogether to use it for professional reasons. Paper it could deal with, but a Gestetner sheet was a different proposition altogether. For those brought up with PCs and printers it is probably impossible to imagine just what exactly a Gestetner sheet was. It was like a dishcloth that you have just used to wipe all the surfaces in the kitchen – slimy, slippery, and distinctly smelly. It was grey and the texture was a cross between an old sock and a used condom. Loading it onto a typewriter was like trying to push a worm through a keyhole.

When you had eventually managed to load the Gestetner sheet into the typewriter without ripping it or breaking your nails, you then had to position the sheet neatly and evenly so that when reproduced it didn't look as if some drunken spider had scrawled across the page. The typist then had to type out the Foreign Words and the typewriter keys cut into the Gestetner sheet and produced the text. It was rather like the Enigma machines used by the German army during the Second World War. And just as effective. The code breaking required after one sheet had been produced by an inexpert typist in about three hours would have defeated most of the Bletchley Park team for several months.

Of course if the typist made a single mistake then he would be severely punished. Guilty again. It really was good for the soul. A mistake would have to be obliterated with a vile red liquid smelling like nail varnish and the mistake would have to be retyped over the offending word. This meant that after I had managed fitfully and painfully to type a worksheet for the Third Form, the resulting Gestetner sheet would look as though it was covered in angry red blotches that underscored my guilt and emphasised my status as one of the Lost. One colleague, noticing over my shoulder a recently savaged sheet, wondered if I had slit my wrists whilst composing 3Z's half-term test.

With the Gestetner sheet complete, all the tyro-typist-teacher had to do was extract it from the typewriter without shrivelling it into a congealed mess and then take it to the dreaded Printing Machine. Now this machine had been invented in the days when teachers had nothing better to do than spend about half-an-hour trying to transfer a Gestetner sheet with backing carbon paper, red corrections and angry tears onto an ink-stained drum as slippery as a ski slope. It required nerves of steel to get the sheet onto the drum, extract the carbon paper, wipe the permanent ink from one's hands and fingers and sleeves and cheek, prime the ink (pump furiously until it squirts all over the place except onto the rollers), load the paper, turn the handle ever so slowly so that all of the sheet is covered and so that the ink is evenly spread across the virgin paper and the Foreign Words text is clear and ready to be deciphered. What I usually got was a mangled sheet of shredded text.

If there was too much ink, the worksheet resembled a Jackson Pollock painting on an off day; or if there was too little ink then the sheet had the merest hint of text, an Impressionist vision of foggy London town; or else the sheet somehow managed to screw itself up as it turned in the infernal machine and this attempt rivalled

Dadaist poetry at its best: odd disjointed words randomly spaced across the page.

But the Gestetner was a Rolls Royce when compared with the Banda machine. The Banda was the workhorse of the teaching profession and the glazed look and distracted air of teachers *d'un certain âge* can almost certainly be attributed to the side effects of daily contamination with this industrial hazard. If miners had their coal dust and factory workers had exposure to asbestos, teachers also faced a peril of equal danger. Before the days of Health and Safety, the Banda was always stored in an airless cupboard with about enough room to accommodate one teacher at a time from amongst the usual frantic horde trying to get their worksheets ready at the start of day.

The Banda solvent in essence was a common substitute for drugs. Teachers knew this. Senior management knew this. The Government knew this, but realised that it was an excellent way to keep the profession docile and unwilling to get uppity. Daily access to the Banda was enough to make even the most radical Trotskyist roll over and accept yet another increase in taxation. Many now attribute growing teacher union militancy in the 1980s to the demise of the Banda and reliance on hazard-free worksheet production. Pupils also benefited vicariously because of the lingering after-glow of the Banda weed on the worksheets.

The Banda machine was a drum onto which teachers could fasten a worksheet *that had been written by hand.* The precious Banda fluid, nowadays easily classified as a class A drug (there is a clue in the name: spirit duplicator) was poured in, and the vapours would fill the cupboard. Anyone who had not passed out within five seconds was deemed fit to teach. The benefit of this over the Gestetner was immediately apparent. A worksheet could be hurriedly scribbled off between assembly and registration (in multiple colours), the teacher could get a fix in the Banda cupboard and the pupils could get dosed up in lesson one and so remain quiescent for most of the morning.

It was noticeable how many pupils who did not have their Banda fix in period one showed distinct signs of withdrawal symptoms during morning break and needed to get high in another way, usually through nicotine, alcohol or bullying First Formers to hand over their stock of Banda worksheets.

The advantages of the Banda machine over such trivial modern inventions such as the interactive whiteboard are legion:

- There is no need for electricity
- There is no need for training
- There is no book entitled "Banda worksheets for dummies"
- There are no Banda nerds

- It is cheap
- It is quick
- It is silent
- It does not crash

The solvent alone is worth the cost in order to provide a docile workforce, happy pupils and a balanced budget.

Chapter 6

The exchange trip – first leg: away

Gun metal grey. A strong breeze getting up and the swell beginning to increase. The English coastline was fast disappearing into the distance and I took one last look at my beloved country. In the middle of the Channel everything looked so far away and the dim light did not help. I could just make out the white cliffs, standing supreme and sure, a reminder of why I was on this boat in the first place and it brought a lump to my throat.

The boat was beginning to heave in the swell and I felt distinctly queasy. I looked around. Packed into a tiny space were twenty-two people, all looking grimly at the shoreline they could barely make out. They were squashed together and could scarcely move. There was a peculiar smell. Part body odour, part damp clothing and part the collective fart of all those bodies releasing unnamed gases. Should have brought the Chemistry teacher along. He would have had a field day.

Each was lost in his own thoughts and I could tell from a quick scan of the pinched faces that this journey was going to be like no other that they had been on in their lives before. Their last meal had been in England and just the thought of it made me almost heave up. There is nothing like a good English breakfast to get you going, but I had declined the offer. One piece of toast was enough for me. Out on the open sea, the greasy bacon and congealed egg that most had eaten lay heavy on their stomachs and reminded me that what goes down on land invariably comes up at sea. Trying to take my mind off such unpleasant thoughts I looked at each face in turn. Some had clearly suffered the same meal and were going to find out sooner or later the truth of my own sentiments. Others had a far off look in their eye and were already turning their faces to the direction the boat was heading. One or two seemed to be praying, but on closer inspection I concluded that they were involved in some elaborate personal ritual involving a handkerchief and a sick bag.

It was 4am, the traditional time for such manoeuvres. Move at dawn. Get going before it lightens. Get out on the sea and catch everyone unawares. No time now for second thoughts. No time to reconsider or wish that I had responded to a different calling or a different service. Halfway there. Behind lay the warmth and security of England with all its certainties, all its fog and bacon and eggs and warm beer and cricket and white cliffs and unremitting gloom and ahead lay the Continent with all its uncertainties and dangers and foreignness.

As I contemplated what lay ahead I suddenly caught sight of one of the group who convulsed and fell to the deck. Pushing my way through the others I finally caught up with the prone figure. It was Paul Kelly.

"Are you all right," I asked in that half-interested way that betrayed my lack of real concern.

"Aargh. I can't breathe. Shit. Uurgh." He gasped.

Remembering my hazy first aid course of many years ago, I quickly assessed whether an emergency tracheotomy would be necessary. This particular manoeuvre had greatly impressed me on the course. I had found all that work with bandages and triangular slings and recovery position baffling and mildly ridiculous but the tracheotomy procedure had caught my imagination and I often wondered when I would be called upon to use it.

Maybe it was the reference to doctors being called out on planes to rescue some famous film star who was having breathing difficulty, or maybe it was the thought of saving a glamorous life on a Mediterranean cruise or maybe because it simply involved the use of a ballpoint pen.

As a teacher I had dozens of ballpoint pens, mostly leaking and creating unwelcome and dubious stains on jackets or at the bottom of a briefcase, but at least I now knew that one of them could be a life saver.

All you had to do was make an incision in the throat of the victim, extract the plastic tubing from the ballpoint pen, blow out all the ink, insert it into the throat and hey presto, the victim would be able to breathe through the opening created. Gasps of wonderment from all onlookers. Interview on the Today programme. Article in the Guardian. Celebrity lifestyle thereafter. Probable medal at the Palace.

Whilst lost momentarily in such reverie, I was brought back to earth by the comments of one of Paul's friends.

"He's only swallowed a stink bomb, sir"

The collective fart. The stink bomb. The connection was instantly made and the visit to the Palace instantly evaporated.

"He was just trying to lick the stink bomb and then stick it onto Gary's back when the boat lurched and he swallowed it instead."

"Uurgh," from Paul. "I am going to die."

Assuring him that that was the least of his worries, I managed to get him onto his feet, drag him into the toilet and make him swallow enough water to bring about the desired vomit.

That wasn't part of the first aid course. It also wasn't part of my training. But it seemed to have the desired effect. Most decisions to do with sorting out the misdemeanours of pupils were taken in an instant, without regard for any theory or training or cool reflection. It summed up the teacher's motto: if in doubt, just do it.

With that little episode behind me and with another hour to go before landing at Calais, I cast my mind back to the start of the journey. The Head had reassured me that taking eighteen pupils to France for a fortnight would be a delight and indeed an educational experience for all concerned. I would be accompanied by three Sixth Formers who could be relied on in a tight spot.

Getting on the train in Leeds several hours earlier I had already felt a knot in my stomach tightening. Was it the fish and chips and mushy peas I had had for lunch? Or was it the thought of taking all these pupils on their first trip to France and how I would survive the experience without prematurely ageing.

As the journey had progressed my stomach pains had taken a turn for the worse and I had had to spend a considerable amount of time standing outside the toilet. I could not go into the toilet of course because the door was broken and the toilet seat had been removed (presumably for safe keeping). It was also permanently engaged by a drunken soldier who was still looking for a fight and I didn't want to give him any excuse.

So I obstipated for a large part of the journey, so much so that my obstipation turned to constipation and remained like that for a considerable time.

The first task on arrival into London was to herd the pupils from Kings Cross down into the Underground and across the capital to Victoria Station. There we would catch the train to Dover and then the ferry to Calais.

Straightforward enough. Count them all down the escalator, count them all onto the Tube, put one Sixth Former at the front, one in the middle and one at the rear.

By the time we got into the train I was sweating profusely. My large olive green suitcase (a wedding gift – unused for five years – from a maiden aunt who had never travelled outside Tunbridge Wells) felt like a ton of bricks. It was propped against my leg, which was beginning to go numb. The suitcase had no wheels – of course, this was still the dark ages. There was a large strap holding it together, an entirely inadequate chunky handle with just enough room to get your hand through and then squash it against the suitcase. My stomach began to heave and rumble like a bucket of crabs trying to practise scrummaging. I gripped the handrail and felt my legs start to wobble uncontrollably.

We had arrived at the next station and the doors opened. A blast of hot, dusty air hit my face just as I was trying to count the pupils once again. Why did they keep changing places? Why couldn't they just stand still? Why were they moving around so much?

However, my eyes began to mist over and I felt my stomach churning again. Only this time, the churning was not to be ignored. There was a sickly sensation at the back of my throat, a tremor running up and down my arms and a queasiness welling up in my mouth. I knew I had about five seconds before I was going to be violently sick.

Catching the eye of a Sixth Former, Peter, I shouted: "Get them to Victoria!" and then jumped off the train just as the doors were closing.

I ran towards the exit but before I had gone a few feet, my stomach decided that it had had enough. I lurched, belched and suddenly there was a stream of vomit pouring out of my mouth and onto the station platform.

Worried passengers gave me a wide berth and scurried past. A large gap appeared where only a few minutes previously there had been a milling crowd.

The vomit kept coming, but I hardly cared. The pent up anxiety, the half digested food, the stomach in turmoil and the shaking limbs all combined to produce a torrent of slimy gunk that emanated from my mouth. It lasted about two minutes, but felt like an eternity and at the end of it I was dazed and light-headed with relief. I had not felt so relieved since throwing up magnificently at the end of a four mile cross-country run all over the Headmaster's shoes. The memory of that sensation came back as I tried to steady myself, stand upright and not appear like a midday drunk.

There were streaks of vomit on my jacket and trousers; my shoes were covered in a vile greasy substance and I had a taste of toast, fish, peas and marmalade in my mouth.

After the luxury of only a few minutes post-nausea ecstasy, I took stock of my situation. I had been left alone by all (which was a small mercy) and no-one approached to offer help, to see if I was all right or to arrest me.

I couldn't do anything about the mess I had left behind as I distanced myself as fast as possible from the smelly goo. I slowly came to my senses and began to wonder what I was doing in this distressed state on the London Underground.

Sick. Train. Pupils. Not amused. Victoria!

Bloody hell! I had just abandoned a group of pupils in the heart of London and probably my career at the same time.

In a growing state of panic and alarm, I quickly made my way along the platform and caught the next train to Victoria. As we trundled along I tried to clean myself up by wiping an old newspaper up and down my sleeve and over my trousers and shoes. This gave me even more the appearance of a drunk, especially as most of the newsprint stuck onto my clothing.

The train pulled into Victoria Underground and I rushed up to the mainline station and then over to the platform where the train for the ferry was due. Not thinking about how I would look to the pupils or anyone else for that matter (a smelly, dirty, vomit-smeared, with bits of newspaper stuck on jacket, shambling down-and-out) I noticed a group of youngsters hanging around the cigarette kiosk.

Running and counting (one, two….six, seven) at the same time, I was handing my resignation to the Head and explaining to the local paper just how I managed to abandon all these pupils in London (…….twelve, thirteen…) and how I would spend the rest of life looking after distressed donkeys at a sanctuary in the Western Highlands (……seventeen, eighteen!!). Stuff the donkeys!

Almost weeping with relief, and feeling much like Stanley as he approached Livingstone, I saw Peter, just as he was furtively handing out several packets of fags to the other pupils.

"Well done, Peter. Thanks so much for getting everyone here."

With a few moment's hesitation about being accosted by a drunk covered in vomit, Peter suddenly recognised me, and said,

"That's all right, sir. If you had wanted a drink before getting to Victoria, you only had to say so."

Ignoring his feeble attempt at wit, I tried to focus on the matter in hand and also get myself cleaned up before the next stage of the journey.

"The train for Dover leaves in about 25 minutes so, I think, so I'll nip into the toilet and have a wash." As he opened his mouth to inquire further about my state, I stopped him in his tracks with a firm "I'll explain later."

"Now, Peter, did someone bring my suitcase?"

"What suitcase, sir?"

"You know, that dirty great green thing covered in straps. I had it with me on the...." and that sinking feeling returned with a vengeance.

I was not going to be sick this time. I was not going to embarrass myself in front of all these pupils who had now gathered round and were staring at their French Teacher. I was not going to panic. I was going to have a heart attack and die.

Right. This is just what I had not been prepared for during my PGCE course.

We had learned about Bernstein and Chomsky and Skinner. We had done role plays and simulations. We had explored mixed-ability teaching and streaming. We had even seen "*Kes*".

But we had not done "how-the-bloody-hell-do-I-retrieve-my-suitcase-from-God-knows-where-in-less-than-25-minutes-whilst-not-losing-eighteen-pupils-in-London-and-looking-like-a-drunken-slob-and-still-make-the-train-to-Dover?"

Of course it wasn't just my suitcase containing all my clothes for two weeks. It also contained my passport and several hundred French francs.

Eschewing the easy way out and dying, I quickly assessed the situation.

"Peter. I have to go and find my suitcase. If I am not back in time, get all the pupils to Dover and I'll get myself there somehow. Will explain all later." It could have been an exciting war film, with me as the lead role going off to carry out some amazingly daredevil adventure. As if.

And with that, I turned and made my way down towards the Underground again. I just caught sight of Peter and the two other Sixth Formers handing round the fags, as I descended into hell.

25 minutes. Panic can do amazing things to the human brain. I don't know how many synapses were being fired up as I raced down the escalator two steps at a time. I quickly fathomed that if my suitcase had remained on the train and no-one had nicked it (thank you so much Aunty Ruth for such a tasteless olive green monstrosity) it would have journeyed to the end of the line. As we were travelling from Kings Cross to Victoria that would have been Brixton – only four stops away. I jumped on the next train and got to Brixton in about four minutes. 21 minutes left.

Where on earth do you look for a suitcase in an Underground station? At night. It was by now 9.30pm and the train for Dover left Victoria at 9.51pm. They didn't have any Lost Property departments and there was no indication of just where I should look. In any case they would be closed at this time of night. In desperation I headed for the Station Manager's office and just hoped (a) that it would be open and (b) that I could gain some useful information there.

I had had no time to clean up and was still smelling of old sick, which was now caked onto my jacket and trousers, with bits of newspaper hanging off like grimy confetti.

I was for once in luck. It was open. I pushed the door and before I could say a word glanced down behind the reception desk. There, in the corner, like some long lost friend, was my suitcase! I quickly told the man behind the counter that that was my suitcase and could I please collect it now as I had a train to catch.

Looking at me with a mixture of scorn, disdain and pity, said man behind the counter replied:

"I'm sorry, sir. You can't just walk in here and claim property that has been brought in by Special Branch. We have a few questions to ask."

Special Branch? What on earth could Special Branch want with my tatty green suitcase?

Then it dawned on me. There had been a number of terrorist attacks in London recently and they were taking no liberties with packages or parcels left lying around. Especially in stations. Especially on trains.

"But, I can assure you that that is my suitcase," I stammered. "I am a Teacher" - and what an existential nanosecond that turned out to be. A teacher. A guide to modern youth. A sage. A guru. One to lead others to knowledge and understanding. An upright citizen worthy of admiration and respect and a half decent salary (in your dreams – but we weren't in it for the money). But all the man behind the counter could see was a drunk in shabby smeared clothing ranting on about a suitcase.

Appealing to his better nature, I quickly thought up all the ways that I could convince him of the veracity of my story.

"Look, I'll open the case and show you that all there is inside is my passport, clothing, a few books..." Not a flicker of interest. I could see that I was getting nowhere and time was running out. 15 minutes to go.

Then, in a flash of inspiration, I said "... and of course I have piles of marking to do and it is all in the case."

This seemed to do the trick. A conman would have tried to bribe him with a promise of a new watch or bottle of whisky; a real terrorist would have probably drawn a gun and threatened him. But what was it about teachers that made them stand out from the rest of the population?

They were obsessed with marking. They always had marking to do and it would never cease. They were so obsessed that they even stuffed green suitcases full of it and took it abroad to mark when they were supposed to be on holiday.

He softened and looked at me now not with scorn, nor disdain but just pity.

"Well, sir, if you could just verify that this case does belong to you I am sure that we can let you go on your way."

I almost kissed him. But refrained. Discretion was the better part. I opened the case and showed him the clothes, the books, the passport and, yes, eighteen folders of six pages of A4 paper each.

"Well, that all seems to be in order, sir. If you would just sign here, and here and here, you can take the case and be on your way."

I signed there and there and there and didn't even read what I was signing.

I put the passport in my pocket and closed the case, now with all the clothing and books and papers all jumbled up, I was about to make a somewhat facetious remark about my appearance, lack of Irish accent and futility of the whole exercise, when I thought better of it and walked briskly away.

I now had 11 minutes to go to make it back to Victoria to catch the train to Dover.

My career was once again hanging by a thread, but I was thankful that if I had learned precious little during my own schooldays, the one thing I had learned was that when confronted by authority in any guise, just make up a story. Any story. And the eighteen exchange trip information folders that I had prepared for the pupils worked a treat.

I gripped the suitcase, jumped on the next Tube train and hurtled from Brixton to Stockwell to Vauxhall to Pimlico to Victoria.

Dashing up the escalator, I now had but four minutes to find the group and herd them onto the train. Peter had done his job though and as I raced towards the platform I could see him waving from the train and shouting:

"Can you get us some more Woodbines, sir, we've used up our spare supplies."

I heaved myself and the suitcase onto the train, thanked Peter profusely amid promises of Gauloises and bottles of wine, counted all the bobbing heads, put the case at the end of the compartment and sank into my seat. The train pulled out of the station.

Adrenalin can do funny things to the body. I had not eaten since lunch and it was now nearly 10pm. I had also not drunk anything and this was many years before we became obsessed with carrying bottles of water around with us. My blood-sugar level must have been near zero.

I tried not to think about the scene on the Underground platform. My stomach had not really recovered and was still wrestling with ferrets and squirrels.

Pupils came by and kindly offered me sausage rolls and meat paste sandwiches so lovingly prepared by their mothers, but I declined, firmly yet graciously. I just about managed a packet of crisps (plain) and a cup of weak tea.

The journey to Dover was relatively uneventful and my spirits began to brighten when we turned up at the dockside and could smell the sea. It was now midnight and the ferry wasn't due to leave till 3.30am. We had booked this ferry partly for reasons of economy and partly so that we could arrive in Calais nice and fresh and ready for our *petit déjeuner*. The ferry crossing took about 50 minutes in those days and the night-time route added a certain spice to the adventure.

So we dragged all our luggage into the small café at the ferry terminal and spent the next three hours whiling away the time before the ferry left. The pupils all decided that just what they needed at that moment – like prisoners before execution – was one last big meal. A full English – because it would be two weeks of croissants and chocolate before they could taste a proper breakfast again.

I sat down with Peter and the other Sixth Formers and counted the pupils again. All there. Not bad. Despite the traumas in London we had all arrived and not lost anyone.

"Sir, sir", came an anxious voice from behind me. It was Paul Kelly. "Sir, I haven't got a passport."

Did my ears deceive me or did I just hear someone saying that he hadn't got a passport? Was this someone the same person who had attended two lunchtime briefing sessions about how exceedingly important it was to have all documentation with you before we left England and that certainly included a passport.

This was my second opportunity to have a heart attack and I flunked it again. I must have been revived by the packet of crisps because with Zen-like calm I refrained from strangling him on the spot. It was also too late to remind him of his fecklessness.

Before I even had a chance to say anything, he piped up again:

"My dad said that he couldn't get one before we left and any case Greeny'll get you one. That's his job."

That's right. That's my job. Not only did I have the pleasure of introducing his son to the intricacies and delights of the French language, I also took him away for two weeks for no other reason than it was my job. I also coached Paul in the U15 cricket XI and was his form tutor.

I was his teacher.

And now that included wet-nursing.

Deciding that getting a passport at midnight couldn't be any more difficult than rescuing my suitcase from Special Branch, I asked Peter to look after the remaining seventeen whilst I took Paul off towards HM Customs & Excise.

Fortunately the forces of law and order were working round the clock and didn't consider myself or Paul a terrorist threat. I took special delight at ringing Mr Kelly at 12.30am so that he could confirm his son's identity and satisfy HM Customs & Excise that he had a legitimate excuse to be leaving the UK and, more importantly, that he had "right of abode" in the UK.

Funny word "abode". I could only think of two occasions when the verb "to abide" was ever used in the English language. "Abide with me" at the FA Cup Final and "right of abode" on passports. Why I was having such thoughts at 12.30am in Dover about to board a ferry to France remains a mystery and goes further to explain the inner workings of a teacher's mind.

The paperwork was duly checked, signed for and an emergency passport issued.

We went back to join the others in the café and awaited the departure of the ferry. I managed to get some sleep – with strange dreams involving vomiting into the FA Cup and being chased down a railway line by screaming fans – and awoke at about 2.45am, just in time to board the ferry.

I counted all the pupils again and herded them into a group so that we could all embark together. I found the group booking ticket and my passport and we all prepared for the adventure that lay ahead.

At 3am we scrambled on board and the pupils immediately made for the bar and an opportunity to light up. I was past caring and just wanted to find a quiet corner where I could sit and hopefully go to sleep for half an hour or so.

We were due to be met by our French counterparts on our arrival in Calais and I looked forward to getting shot of the pupils to their host families as fast as possible and then crawling into bed and hiding away from everyone for about a week.

At 3.30am the ferry moved away from the harbour and we were bound for the Continent and two weeks of exchange trip fun and games.

I relaxed and closed my eyes. And so I could not have seen that there, left on the quayside, was one large olive green suitcase.

Chapter 7

Doing words and describing words.

The eternal paradox of teaching is the inability of explanation to do its job and the atavistic urge of teachers to explain.

Who was the first teacher? Was it the one who noticed others daubing woad happily on the walls of the cave and went over and, instead of joining in and having some fun getting all blue and sticky, asked in a condescending yet mildly interested way:

"So, Zog, what did you have in mind when you sploshed that bit of woad onto that bison looking animal? Was it an artistic statement about the angst of experience and the daily struggle for life or an attempt to portray the intensity of your emotions when seeing the sunset? To get a level five in Creative Cave Art and Design you'll need to show more tone and contrast."

Zog: "Ugh nnegh zrtth yucch."

So no change there then.

What was the motivation for always asking questions? I am reminded of a quotation I saw from a 19th century school classroom in Germany:

"Teachers are those people who help us to solve problems that without them we would never have had."

Ever since time immemorial teachers have asked questions and expected their pupils to come up with the answers. That is the way it is and the way it is meant to be and it is pre-ordained.

The most common question of all is:

"Can you guess what I am thinking?" or its half-brother "Can you see what is in my head?"

Surprisingly, the pupils cannot see, and so blindly shoot in the dark. By the law of averages, someone in most classes can guess what the teacher is thinking on every fifth occasion. So most of the time, teachers don't bother waiting for an answer but simply answer the question themselves. That is a lot quicker and they sometimes get it right.

This is the usual scenario for question and answer sessions that could be repeated in a thousand classrooms up and down the land:

Teacher: "Can anyone guess what I am thinking?"

Pupil: "Toast / grandma / buses / ice-cream / Liverpool / what's for tea tonight?"

Teacher: "Well, to put it another way: what kind of word is "aller"?"

Pupil: (sensing something about words) "a describing word?"

Teacher: "No."

Pupil: "a French word?"

Teacher: "Well done, Malcolm, (thankful for the merest morsel from that quarter) and...?"

Pupil: "a noun / connective / determiner / onomatopoeia / metaphor / simile / alliteration / paragraph ..." (all showing that they did concentrate once during the Literacy Hour)

Teacher: "No. Look, if I say "je vais au garage" and je vais is from aller, what kind of word do you think aller is?"

Pupils hear:

"No. Look if I say blubber mmmurph snnny and blubber is from snoogle what kind of word do you think snoogle is?"

Pupil: (hesitantly) "Sir, is it a ... describing word?"

Teacher: (beginning to despair but valiantly carrying on with the illusion that some communication is taking place) "Well, Jane suggested that some time ago, and it was incorrect" (and thinking – so what the bloody hell do you think happened in the intervening ten minutes to transform a wrong answer into a right one? Was the law of gravity suddenly suspended? Did the Second Law of Thermodynamics dramatically become obsolete? Did the English language turn into Japanese?)

Pupil: "I don't get it."

Teacher: (with infinite wisdom and patience gently coaxing out of his young charges pearls of wisdom and insight) "Well, Malcolm, we only did this yesterday, so I rather hoped that you would not need me to go over it once again. What exactly do you not get?"

Now this is another of those teacher questions that is impossible to answer.

One day when Malcolm and Garth were being at their most obtuse and I simply wanted the bell to ring for the end of the lesson, Caitlin decided to launch her Exocet question. This question was the one that all teachers dreaded. It was a question that demanded an answer, but an answer totally beyond the powers of any human being to provide to the satisfaction of the questioner.

It was the kind of question that passengers used to ask frequently of Customer Service Team Leaders on trains:

"Why is this train running late?"

It was the kind of question that consumers would ask of any Helpdesk:

"Why are you called a Help Desk?"

It was the kind of question that any child might ask of its parents on Christmas Eve:

"Why do we put sherry and mince pies in front of the gas fire when we haven't got a chimney?"

It was the kind of question that I heard myself asking on a daily basis to pupils in Year 8:

"Why are you late?"

Caitlin's question was all the more deadly because it came out of the blue from an engaging pupil who was not used to causing trouble and who could usually be relied upon to hand out worksheets, sharpen pencils and not hide the interactive whiteboard pens. With about fifteen minutes to go, I had set the class their final piece of work for the day and they were cheerfully engaged on a pair work activity. There was a hum of chatter as the pupils speculated on the next episode of the current popular soap, the love life of any number of starlets and footballers and which member of Year 8 had been snogged by cool Clive in Year 10. The chatter was just soft enough not to be distracting and loud enough to show that they were all still awake. The task set was undemanding enough so that they could have a reasonable stab at it without too much concentration.

I had been facilitating the learning appropriately ("open the book, Mary"), making incisive interventions ("put it away, Tom"), asking pertinent yet challenging questions ("have you got a pencil, Tracy?") and circulating purposefully. I had just got back to my desk when Caitlin, without putting up her hand, asked in a disinterested way:

"Sir, why did you become a teacher?"

The pupils froze. It was one of those brilliant disarming questions that teachers could not complain about. It was not rude, nor facetious. It was asked by one of the more amenable pupils in the class and clearly not a set-up. Even Garth and Malcolm stopped mid-arm-wrestle and turned towards me. If this had been a film it would have been just like the moment when Harrison Ford realises that the bomb will go off if someone opens the car door, and the pretty woman is just about to put her hand to the passenger side and our hero launches himself at her crying "NO!" and the whole picture slows right down and the woman turns slowly, ever so slowly towards him with a look of bewilderment and incomprehension...

I had that look on my face.

The question hung in the air, menacing, accusing and demanding a reply.

Yes, Simon. Why had you become a teacher?

After all, there were no teachers in my family. The last time, and indeed the only time I had been asked that question, was at the interview for my PGCE course twenty something years previously. JJ had asked me in a perfunctory way and I had mumbled something about wanting to contribute to society, pass on my knowledge and love of languages and help youngsters with their education. It didn't sound very convincing then and even less so now. When accepted onto the course I did notice that there were only a few men but a large number of very attractive women. I asked JJ the criteria for selection.

"Very simple, Simon. If a bloke, have they got a good degree and don't look gormless. If a woman, blue eyes and big tits."

Well I knew about my good degree and was relieved about the second criterion. And the other criteria seemed accurate enough too.

Chapter 8

New variant CPD

Can a teacher be trained?

Is teaching one of those activities that is simply a given?

Everyone has been to school and so everyone has experienced teaching in one form or another.

In my quieter moments and when I had time to reflect, I occasionally wondered whether those who had taught me far too many years previously had ever had any kind of training at all. Of course they would never have used the word "training" with its overtones of overalls and engineering and skills and technical capability. Universities, after all, did not have Faculties of Training but rather Faculties of Education or even Schools of Education and when I had taken my PGCE all those years ago it was very much a Certificate in Education and not Training.

My teachers had gone to school, gone on to university to read French or Mathematics or Classics or some other proper subject with a one word name which was instantly recognisable. It was only Oxbridge that liked to keep the mystique of higher learning with Greats and Mods and Tripos so that no-one outside the circle had the faintest idea what on earth you had been doing all that time at Varsity. You went to university to read. I remembered the story of a famous Professor of Education who had been invited to give a lecture to first year undergraduates on the value of revision before major examinations. The eminent professor had been granted an hour for this topic. He mounted the stage, stood behind the lectern, peered at the upturned faces before him and announced in ringing tones: "Open the bloody book!" and sat down.

However, as in the way of all progress, single honours had given way to combined degrees, modular courses, flexible learning, open and optional modules, mix and match degrees so that instead of studying for one single subject students could now opt for courses on Digital Media and the Aesthetics of the Nineteenth Century with optional sports journalism.

My own teachers, having left university, would have gone straight into teaching. Some may have picked up a diploma in education on the way (in the way you tried to get chicken pox out of the way in early childhood) but it was never mentioned, certainly never included in the illustrious qualifications listed after each member of staff in the school prospectus.

My teachers had learnt French with Whitmarsh[3]. They had gone onto university to read French. They may or may not have visited the country and spoken to some

---

[3] WFH Whitmarsh's Complete French Course for First Examinations

sympathetic native speakers. They then returned to school to pick up Whitmarsh's First Book of French (Green cover) and start the process all over again. You learnt the language. You studied it further. You went back and taught the language in the same way. What could be simpler?

Your pupils then made the same mistakes as pupils always did down the centuries and you punished them for their indolence, stupidity and lack of moral fibre in the same way that you had been punished before. Tweaking of ears, plimsolls on bottoms, flying board rubbers, detention and lines all ensured that pupils learnt thoroughly the eternal verities: "the past participle in the *passé composé* must agree with any preceding direct object pronoun"; "*bagages*" has one g in the middle and not two"; "there are 13 verbs which take *être* in the *passé composé* and there is only one way of remembering this fact: DRAPERS VAN MMT". I recalled how amazed I had been to find some students at my university who had not learned this fact in this way but by a more subtle method: MRS VANDETRAMP. This was indeed a Eureka experience. There was more than one way to learn French. Incredible! How could this be?

Training would merely have complicated the issue and implied that the teachers didn't really know what they were doing. The seamless cycle of school to university to school would have been broken.

And then came the comprehensive schools. A new generation was introduced to foreign languages, a generation not used to direct objects of any kind, let alone preceding ones and Whitmarsh was found wanting. Instead of passively accepting all that was offered, some began to ask searching questions about the education they were receiving and found the answers equally wanting: "Sir, why have we got to learn French, it's boring."

"Because it is very useful and you will get a good job and you will be an educated person in the 20th century and you will have knowledge of a great culture and you will be able to travel to far off distant shores and people will understand your every word and you in turn will understand them and there will be mutual tolerance and understanding and the Entente Cordiale will not have been in vain and one day maybe French footballers will come here to ply their trade and we will be able to communicate with them and we will be able to export all our British cars and technology and foodstuffs to France and we will be joint members of a great European enterprise holding back the forces of federalism but playing our part at the centre and you will understand great literature from Voltaire and Molière and Sartre and when you get to university you will be cool because you will have read *Bonjour tristesse* in the original and understand all the pain and anguish of existentialism and you will be able to chat up French girls who will be so impressed by your command of the preceding direct object yet strangely amused by your ever so cute English accent and you will be able to order a meal in a restaurant overlooking the Seine with nonchalance and sang-froid and understand the meaning of nonchalance and sang-froid and why they are important and you will delight in the intellectual challenge of making sense of Baudelaire and have deep pleasure at seeing the double entendres in Beckett or Ionesco and be able to do the Guardian crossword and excel in any pub quiz when the question about the tricolore comes up (as it always does and everyone gets it the wrong way round – it is of course *bleu blanc rouge* - and if you learn your colours properly you will always get that right) and a GCSE in French is a gateway to future success, wealth, happiness and prosperity for all mankind, Kevin."

"It's still boring, sir." (But in fact what Kevin really wants to say is: French is not useful at all and I know no-one in my immediate family or circle of friends who has ever found any use whatsoever for using any word of French at any time and whenever anyone speaking French comes on the TV even if it is the president himself they always dub into English straightaway and even if you do get a really cool film like Amélie they put all the subtitles in English on the bottom and all the footballers and even their managers speak better English than most of the other players in the premiership and I will not go on to university to read all those poncy books 'cos I am going to do sports and personal hygiene and we always go to Lanzarote or Ibiza or Malaga for our holidays and you don't need to speak French there 'cos everyone speaks

English anyway and I don't like French birds anyway – too scraggy and la-di-da and they eat disgusting food and their beer tastes like cat's piss and the Sun crossword doesn't use foreign words and down our pub all the questions are about soaps and football and beer and GCSE is no good for anyone if you get a grade U which I will get 'cos I ain't learned nothing and why can't I do car maintenance instead anyway.)

So when I saw a training course coming up at my Local Education Authority training centre (Woodstock Hall) entitled "Motivating the Reluctant Learner - Ten Winning Ways to Engage the Most Recalcitrant" I thought I would give it a go.

My school was prepared to give me the day off to attend (provided I set work for the six classes I would miss). So I duly prepared a series of worksheets and handouts with copious instructions and left them in the capable hands of a colleague.

Woodstock Hall was one of those grand stately homes that had fallen on hard times and been bought by the LEA (many years later to be streamlined as LA – when would Education cease to be part of the acronym and it become an American city? And when would it transmogrify into simply "L"?) as a venue for training courses. Set in splendid grounds with fine gardens, a croquet lawn, an adjoining leisure centre and golf course and noted for its excellent cuisine, I felt immediately relaxed as I drove down the two mile drive to the entrance. I imagined spending more than one day here, a week perhaps or even a month. I would undertake some research during the morning, have a light lunch, play nine holes of golf, do a little more reading in the afternoon, go for a swim, have a couple of pints and then a fine three course dinner, sit in the opulent lounge and read the papers, do the crossword and join fellow guests for a drink in the bar or a game of snooker perhaps. Now all I needed to do was win the pools.

I joined the queue at the registration desk. As usual, all the other participants were women. Out of the twelve registered for the course I was the only man. This was quite normal and in no way perturbed me. I enjoyed the company of women and it spared me the ritual conversation about football, cars and gadgetry that I usually got in the staffroom.

Collecting my badge and noting once again the inability of the organisation to spell my name correctly (Simone Greene) I went in search of coffee. I knew that the three essential prerequisites of a good training course were parking, toilets and hot coffee. I had found the first two and now needed the third in the sequence to set me up for the day.

Like all modern training establishments, Woodstock Hall had succumbed to the wiles of the marketing, health and safety and quality gurus. On almost every wall there were uplifting posters with whales' tails disappearing into the foaming sea, climbers on mountain peaks, birds soaring in flight and surfers cresting mighty waves. Each was graced with a caption guaranteed to lift your spirit and challenge your mind. "Expand, expend, enhance"; "To be the best, beat the rest"; "Even obstacles just look like doors when seen from the inside"; "A challenge a day keeps your mind in the fray". I hadn't the faintest idea what any of them meant and certainly couldn't see how the whale and the surfer could help me with Wayne and Jimmy. Pondering these insights I now faced my first challenge: how to get a coffee.

In the spirit of "Quality Quik Qoffee" ("The thinking person's drink"), Woodstock Hall had provided hot water flasks and some coffee sachets that looked like a GCSE D&T project (grade U). The sachets were as long and thin as a pencil and designed in three colours: red for "This one's got caffeine in it - are you already tired of living?" blue for "This one's caffeine free and so will taste like lukewarm brown water – but hey, who cares, you want a healthy heart don't you?" and green for "This one is dirt cheap East African caffeine free roasted pecan nut shell gratings – tastes like used cat litter but does your soul good."

I tried to open the last remaining red sachet (eleven other tired of living teachers on the course then) and quickly realised that my search for 3Q heaven might take a little while to come to fruition. The sachet was so thin that any attempt to twist it open or tear off the top was doomed from the outset. I only succeeded in screwing the packet into a tightly constricted foil ball and did not manage to get out any coffee at all. I then tried to tear it open with my teeth and simply got a piece of foil stuck in between my teeth and a sore lip. In frustration I finally pulled both ends as hard as I could until the sachet burst open and showered the whole area in granules of evil caffeine laden coffee. Scraping up as many granules as I could with the wooden spindly lollipop stick ("Colombian Pine Stirring Rod with Scooped Dexterity Handles") and sweeping them off the table into the plastic cup ("Finnish Designed Quality Beverage Qontainer") I then attempted to get some water out of the flask.

Normally a flask would be like a jug which you would upend and pour into your cup. But Woodstock Hall had bought into the Quality market heart and soul and nothing so simple as a jug would ever grace their tables. This was a "Silver Service Pump Action Top Loading Liquid Dispenser". To get hot water out you simply had to pump the lid and the water would flow out smoothly into your cup or FDQBQ. After several pumping attempts that made me seem as if I were auditioning for the part of a deranged medic on some American hospital soap, I managed to extract a few drops of the precious liquid of life onto my gritty granules. Despairing of ever getting a drink, I decided to turn the flask upside down and hope that gravity would still function. Gravity did indeed function and so perfectly that not only did I receive the requisite amount of water in my cup but my cup flowed over with water and the plastic top of the flask and the pump action device inside and eventually the whole flask after I had scalded my hand in the process. Trying to make light of the whole situation, I effortlessly righted the flask, dabbed my scalded hand with some paper towels, and moved away in search of the biscuits. As I did so I caught sight of an uplifting message on the wall behind the table: "Quiet Thoughts are the Product of a Mind at Peace."

The room where the course was to be held had once been an elegant drawing room. It had huge dark burgundy velvet curtains, an immense old fireplace with oak mantelpiece, oak panelled walls, old bookcases and French windows opening onto the croquet lawn. Because the presenter was using PowerPoint the curtains were drawn and there was the gentle hum of fluorescent lighting. There was a flipchart with assorted pens, a portable data projector, free standing screen, computer and trailing cables at one end of a long desk and three tables set out with four chairs to each. The chairs were comfy dining chairs with velvety covers and in front of each there was a pad of headed notepaper ("Woodstock Hall - We Deliver Quality - You Deserve Better"), a monogrammed biro, a name plate (Simone Greene) and three bottles of water – sparkling, still and half-sparkling. Presumably this last one had half as many bubbles as the sparkling. There were also two bottles of brightly coloured liquid – one green and the other orange – industrial strength E numbers to help you through the day. Finally there was a small bowl of sticky boiled sweets.

I sat down and looked around. I didn't recognise anyone else on the course and I was immediately struck by how young they all looked. I couldn't understand how these attractive young women would have any problems motivating the likes of Jimmy and Wayne - but then they would have to learn some French sometime and that would always be the sticking point.

The presenter, Carol Finklestein, came with impeccable references and recommendations from a number of Quality Training Providers (QTPs) - "always delivers in such a way as to leave you wanting", "Carol has the surefire touch of a Quality Presenter – not too much and not too little – in fact hardly anything at all", and "Carol leaves nothing to chance. She packs the day with so much there is scarcely time to breathe".

Carol quickly scanned the ranks of the attendees and welcomed us to the course. Dispensing quickly with the domestics, "fire exits at every corner and no drill planned for today so if you hear a bell, run like hell" she got down to business.

"I want to assure you all," she began, "that this course has been robustly and rigorously planned so that we maximise our synergies and progress our force fields in a win-win situation. Drawing on recent research from a number of the most prestigious universities, I have devised this course around best practice training needs analysis, learning styles, sociolinguistic terminology and dynamic pedagogy. Examples will be taken from real time didactic interactions in the field and underlying assumptions will be thoroughly explored. There will be opportunities for in-depth discussion of appropriate parameters, change agents and behaviour re-modelling as well as an examination of the impact of information technology upon target language usage. All of this is covered in my latest publication (Deadly Serious Publications, £15.99); 'Sod the theory, just tell the little blighters.' "

"So, in keeping with our equal opportunities policy and open access arrangements, I thought we would start with a whole group discussion about the need for such a course as this. Do you want to re-negotiate the agenda? Shall we start with an exploration of our own personality typology or move straight onto the exciting research from the University of Wooloogoola and the influence of birth order upon social deviance amongst adolescents in the outback? What would you all like to do?"

At this point all attendees found their shoes most interesting and I wondered if I had come to the right room. I thought of cover period one when Ms Postlethwaite, the Newly Qualified Teacher of RE (and so only one up the food chain from the teacher trainee) would be looking after the newly nominated Year 8 and trying to explain for the umpteenth time how to do the worksheet I had set. "Look it really is very simple. You just have to match the words on the left with the pictures on the right. So here is "*bleu*" – what do you think that means?" "Volcano, CD player, lion cub, cricket bat..." and the whole cycle would begin all over again until the end of recorded time. Whilst reminiscing thus, I unwisely caught the eye of Ms Finklestein. "So, Simon, gentleman first." Titter all round. "What would you like to contribute to the start of our discussion?"

All eyes turned on me and a ripple of relief spread around the group. Thank goodness she didn't drop on me was the unspoken yet unmistakable message that went from face to face. "Well, I would simply like to know how to get the boys in Year 8 to stop mucking about and learn some French."

There was the merest flicker of panic on the face of Carol Finklestein, but it was so swift and so mere that you would have to have been concentrating very hard on her features to have spotted it. Fortunately for her, all the other attendees were still looking in embarrassment at their nice new pointy shoes, outwardly aghast that someone could ask such an obvious question and inwardly delighted that someone else had. I spotted it.

"If I could just reframe your question, Simon, for the benefit of the rest of the group. I think what Simon is formulating is the quintessence of this course and throughout the day I want us all to focus positively upon the complex dimensions of the issue hereby illuminated. Gender stereotyping is one of the pitfalls of course and we must not simplistically focus on male adolescent bonding patterns. Some recent research coming out of

Estonia does point to cross-gender behavioural interplay around puberty. This interplay, coupled with necessary curricular constraints outlined so succinctly by Simon, nearly always results in negative social down-spiralling. Are you familiar with Pelanovski and Kraminia, Simon?"

Before I had a chance to answer, one of the others suddenly looked up and said: "Pelanovski and Kraminia? Oh we did that last year on our College and School Middle Management course. I thought it very 1970s and superseded by Van der Plank and Krofftski from Budapest. Their take was that although curricular constraints may contribute to social down-spiralling, a much more important factor was the time of day of the lesson, the so-called Chronic Constant."

There's only one Chronic Constant around here, I thought, and it has little to do with Year 8.

"Excellent, Yolanda," enthused Carol, recognising a kindred spirit and one with whom she could now swop eastern European research names like Top Trumps all day. I could already see how the conversation would continue: "I've got a Krabbotch and Wankel — I'll swop you for a Knittel and Kerplunk".

"So, I think we have clarified that issue sufficiently," said Carol, beaming at all the other attendees."

At this point the hotel's air-conditioning system clicked on and we were all treated to a blast of cool air and the sound of a jumbo jet taking off.

Taking her cue, and sensing that she should move on rapidly while she was ahead, Carol jumped forward to her top teaching tips: "Here are my ten winning ways to engage the most recalcitrant:" (with my simultaneous translation into Plebo underneath: Plain English and the Bloody Obvious)

Conduct an in-depth teaching needs analysis of the targeted cohort
(Ask them what they want to know)

Track the pupil performance assessment ratio against the desired learning outcome attainment criteria
(Make sure they learn something useful)

Prepare a high challenge low stress differentiated starter activity
(Play bingo)

Ensure smooth transition to individualised learning agendas via an integrated interactive whiteboard task-based simulation on palettes
(Copy from the board)

Provide an intercultural, multidimensional and plurilingual video streamed authentic listening exposé
(Watch a film)

Enable multitasking in cross-gender multi-ability groupings with co-related peer assessment opportunities
(Play noughts and crosses – boys v girls)

Maximise exposure to authentic lexis and syntactical elements in linear sequencing patterns
(Read)

Facilitate intertextual analysis and transcribe illustrative material
(Do a crossword)

Synthesise itemised categorisation of high frequency phoneme-grapheme correspondences
(Play hangman)

Analyse regular patterns of morphological indices and cross-relate them to indicative forms
(Do a word search)

"Now, I want you all to get into groups of three and prioritise these ten winning ways. Take about an hour over that and we can then feedback a collective response."

I found myself with Yolanda and Pammy, another of Carol's acolytes. After brief introductions, (Yolanda teaching at the Blood of the Cross and Passion Martyrs' High School and Pammy at one of the more ancient and prestigious independent schools, William the Conqueror), we got down to work.

"Well, I just think Carol is amazing," said Pammy. "Her research is always so rigorous and robust and you can't fault her reasoning. I had never thought that morphological indices and intertextual analysis were so crucial to the holistic learning paradigm, but now it all makes sense."

"I agree," said Yolanda. "Apart from that slip up over Pelanovski and Kraminia, I think she is taxonomically sound. Her take on multi-tasking just left me gasping. It was so functionally specific, yet strangely over-arching. What do you think, Simon?"

Both of the true believers turned their sparkling eyes and euphoric gazes upon me. Wrapped up in their adoration of the Wise One, they could only look in pity on this poor old man who had presumably wandered into their territory seeking a warm drink and a read of the newspapers. His simplistic question had immediately marked him out as an Unbeliever and One To Be Watched. Very 1950s and probably still believed in giving pupils vocab tests and other dubious heretical practices.

What I wanted to say and what I actually said differed only by a word. And yet the impact could scarcely have been any less if I had stripped off there and then and performed a rugby Haka, tongues and all.

What I wanted to say was:

"I haven't heard such a load of old bollocks since Professor Gross gave us the benefit of his wisdom during my PGCE year by regaling us with Tales of the Raj teaching English grammar to the local population."

What I actually said was:

"I haven't heard such a load of old cobblers since Professor Gross gave us the benefit of his wisdom during my PGCE year by regaling us with Tales of the Raj teaching English grammar to the local population."

Yolanda and Pammy shifted a few feet away and stared at each other uneasily. How could they cleanse themselves from contact with such an unbeliever yet maintain a certain professional decorum? Yolanda decided to ask Carol to join the group so that she could engage directly with the infidel in their midst.

I realised that I had as much chance of discussing the points raised rationally and in a civilised manner as trying to persuade two Jehovah's Witnesses that the Watchtower is the hero's fortress in the Adventures of He-Man.

When the group work was concluded, we re-formed into a biddable group of pseudo-trainees and awaited our tutor's wise words.

Carol began warming to her theme. She could tell early on that there were eleven disciples and one MAAF (Mr Angry-Arms Folded). She knew from experience that she simply needed to keep the disciples on her side and isolate the awkward man.

I had to admire her strategy and also her complete confidence in her own ability. There was not a scintilla of doubt in her presentation, no other possible way of analysing the situation. She had her ideology and she was not going to let mere facts get in the way of a good theory.

Like a priest taking wide-eyed youngsters through their first catechism, she reeled off a question and answer session on "The end of education" without expecting any dissent, any questions or any comment.

Catechism/Lesson First: On the End of Education

Q   Who made the world?
God made the world.

Q   Who is God?
God is the Creator of heaven and earth, and of all things.

Q   What is God's agent of education on earth?
God's agent of education on earth is The Department.

Q   What is The Department?

The Department knows all things, sees all things, decides all things and is never knowingly undersold.

Q   What is the role of The Department?
The role of The Department is to ensure compliance in all things, to devise ever more complicated procedures to maintain a pretence of progress, to massage statistics in such a way that no one understands them any more, to pour scorn on all research that contradicts their stated aims, to feed the Daily Mail with alarming stories about trendy teachers in order to support the Independent Sector.

Q   What is the Independent Sector?
Schools for the offspring of Daily Mail readers.

Q   How does The Department ensure compliance?
The Department ensures compliance by unleashing the forces of Ofsted upon all institutions in order to name and shame them into submission.

Q   What is Ofsted.
Ofsted is the Office of the Holy Inquisition.

Q   What must we do to save our souls?
To save our souls, we must worship The Department by faith, hope and charity; that is, we must believe in The Department, hope in The Department, and love The Department with all our heart.

Q   How shall we know the things which we are to believe?

We shall know the things which we are to believe from the blizzard of initiatives, through which The Department speaks to us.

Q   Where shall we find the chief truths which The Department teaches?

We shall find the chief truths which The Department teaches in the Teachers' Creed.

Q   Say the Teachers' Creed.

I believe in The Department, Creator of quality, standards and efficiency on earth; and in Ofsted, its only Son, who was conceived by the mysterious actions of ministers, born of the Tory Party, suffered teachers to come unto it, crucified them, and they descended into hell.   On the Thursday, under New Labour, Ofsted ascended into heaven, and sitteth at the right hand of The Department, from thence it shall come to judge the living and the dead on their feet.

I believe in the National Curriculum, school performance tables and SATs, the forgiveness of spin, the resurrection of the shoddy, and assessment everlasting. Amen.

Lesson Second: On the Department and its perfections

Q   Had The Department a beginning?

The Department had no beginning; it always was and it always will be.

Q   Where is The Department?
The Department is everywhere.

Q   If The Department is everywhere, why do we not see it?
We do not see The Department, but it is seen in a million missives, a thousand initiatives and in the faces of its compliant minions.

Q   What is the outward and visible sign of The Department?
The outward and visible sign of The Department is the face of every teacher preparing for Ofsted.

Lesson Third: On the unity and trinity of the Department

Q   Is there but one Department?
Yes, there is but one Department.

Q   Why can there be but one Department?
There can be but one Department, because The Department, being supreme and infinite, cannot have an equal.

Q   How many Parts are there in The Department?
In The Department there are three Parts, really distinct, and equal in all things — Quality, Standards and League Tables.

Q   Is Quality The Department?
Quality is The Department and the first Part of the Blessed Trinity.

Q   Are Standards The Department?
Standards are The Department and the second Part of the Blessed Trinity.

Q   Are League Tables The Department?
League Tables are The Department and the third Part of the Blessed Trinity.

Q   What is the Blessed Trinity?
The Blessed Trinity is one Department in three Parts.

Q   Are the three Parts one and the same Department?
The three Parts are one and the same Department.

Q   Does Quality always get better?
Quality always gets better because The Department says it does.

Q   Do standards always improve?
Standards always improve because The Department says they do.

Q   Do league tables show consistent performance over a long period and are reliable indicators of a school's academic record, a guide to the competence of teaching staff and an accurate portrayal of pupils' progress against statistically significant and reliable data?

Yes. God help us.

And that is the end of education.

Chapter 9

The cover lesson

I had often wondered about how cover lessons were distributed and how it was that whichever day of the week my solitary "free" lesson fell would be the same day that someone fell ill or had to attend one of Carol Finklestein's inspiring sessions. Luck was a strange commodity. Not only did I never get enough draws in the football pools, usually I was lucky if I managed one draw at all. In fact the likelihood of winning the pools was probably only slightly diminished by the fact that I only ever did the pools twice a year. I turned back to my marking and away from the luxury villa in the Dordogne.

Cover lessons – the universal term for substitute lessons – covering for an absent colleague, providing appropriate empathetic support for a fellow teacher in distress, more likely covering up for a malingering bastard who always arrived late, left early and somehow failed to turn up to relieve you after an hour's invigilation in the freezing sports hall in January (oh ever so sorry I thought it said 3pm in the Art Room - ie warm, dry and with tea and cakes provided – and when I got there the three (female) Sixth Form Art students were painting a still life and I had to supervise them very closely for an hour) – were the universal bane of every teacher's life.

If I were to make a list of Universal Banes of teachers' lives, this is what it would look like:

Cover lessons
Doing an assembly
Report writing
Marking anything anywhere at anytime for any reason at all ever
Being a marker for cross country
Serving tea at Open Evening
Open Day (with charity collection) – giving the children a legitimate excuse to piss you off, make fun of you, humiliate you, cover you in baked beans, and then charge you for the privilege
Parents who are teachers
Parents who don't come to parents' evenings
Parents who come to parents' evenings
Younger headteachers
Older Foreign Language Assistants
When the chalk disappears (pre circa 1970)
When the Banda fluid runs out (pre circa 1980)
When the Gestetner thingy gets wrapped around the drum (pre circa 1990)
When the floppy disk is corrupted (pre circa 2000)
When the interactive whiteboard pens mysteriously disappear (21st century)
When the chalk runs out (2020)

And so it was that Thursday afternoon, the slot of death just after lunchtime, when my one remaining free period was swallowed up by a cover lesson.

I quickly calculated the exact mathematical formula in my mind:

Second Form[4] + windy day +just after lunch + RE cover lesson = hell.

It is a universal fact and well known to all teachers that there is a direct correlation between weather and behaviour. Whatever the weather, the behaviour is bad. However, windy days seem to take behaviour to a different dimension altogether. During the full moon, some pupils exhibit behaviour normally only seen in celebrity TV shows. When it snows, everyone joins in the fun, including the head who promptly bans snowball fights and making snowmen. When it is windy then all of the pupils go wild. It is as if their DNA is linked subliminally to some weird meteorological trigger that ignites madness at the slightest puff of wind. The resultant behaviour patterns can be tracked against the Beaufort scale:

Calm / Fidgeting

Light Air / Gentle pushing and shoving

Light Breeze / Harder pushing and shoving

Gentle Breeze / GBH

---

[4] Second Form: Old English for Year 8

Moderate Breeze / Desks knocked over

Fresh Breeze / Chairs, desks and other furniture knocked over

Strong Breeze / Rugby match in classroom

Near Gale / Normal Second form* (* see footnote again)

Moderate Gale / Normal second form* with a tantrum (*ditto)

Strong Gale / Time to send for the Deputy Head

Storm / Time to send for the Head

Violent Storm / Time to send for the police

Hurricane / Time to send for the SAS

I turned up at the classroom five minutes in advance and found a haven of tranquillity. Ms Postlethwaite, the RE teacher, had left clear instructions for the 45 minute lesson in her impeccably neat handwriting on her desk.

Second Form (* you know by now): Period 6: Thursday. Religious Education

Lesson planning proforma: 2PQXJ

Resources: flipchart paper / marker pens / cassette recorder / cassette of Bach's St Matthew Passion / sheets of lined paper and pens

Rites of Passage – lesson three

Objectives:

Children should learn:

- to reflect on what they have understood from the course of study
- to attempt their own answer to the question of the meaning of life

Lesson activities

Pupils could play *Just a minute* in teams on rites of passage, drawing on the knowledge and understanding they have developed through their study, *eg pupils have to talk for one minute **on Confirmation** without hesitation or repetition.*

Ask pupils to listen to a piece of music and think about what each of the religions they have studied would say life is about. Then ask pupils to reflect on what they believe life is about. Ask them to draw a diagram/picture to illustrate what these religions would say the meaning of life is, and also to add their own response.

Analyse what they have understood from the course of study and respond with their own answer to the question: *What is the meaning of life*?

Finish off for homework.

I was aghast. The primary principle for a cover lesson was that you provided the class with a bog-standard easy worksheet that required no explanation and let the poor cover teacher get on with some marking. It was a gross career limiting activity if any cover teacher was required to actively participate in actually teaching any lesson. It was the great Unwritten Rule: do unto other cover teachers as you would wish that you were so done unto yourself, and I clearly felt done at the moment.

Not only could I not mark the pile of books I was carrying, but I also could not prepare for lesson 7 which followed and which also was for another second form* (* yeah, yeah...) class.

Of course I could not expect Ms Postlethwaite to understand all of the unwritten rules of the profession. She had only been in the job for five minutes, well seven years, and she was already an Advisory Teacher for the LEA. This meant that she got a whole day off a week for out-reach and in-reach. I wasn't quite sure which was the more painful, suffice it to say that she seemed not to be in school very much and spent a lot of time with clipboards, pie-charts and displayed a faintly bemused air.

I now had four minutes to locate the correct place on the cassette (years of teaching French had taught me how to do this most expertly), and try to work out a seating plan.

The lesson essentially boiled down to:

Game of *Just a minute* in teams.
Listen to music
Draw a picture.
Decide meaning of life.

Much like any other lesson then. So that's OK. During the next lesson with the second form* (*just deal with it) I had planned something similar. Except there would be no game. Nor music. Nor decisions about the meaning of life. But they would draw a picture. Of their bedroom + five favourite objects. And label them. In French. That would do very nicely and would easily take up 45 minutes.

The second form* (*no comment) arrived. The wind had happily abated and was only at a sub-GBH scale and so I thought things were picking up. First I had to deal with the normal light-hearted banter and witty repartee from the class wags:

"Oh, sirrr. Not you. It's doss with Pos."
"RE sucks."
"Why can't we do *Zigger Zagger*?"
"I hate RE. It's boring"

"Where's Pos – she's never here on Thursdays"

Having dealt swiftly with these charming asides, I split the class up into eight groups of four and announced the first lesson objective.

"We (inclusive language) are going to (intention clear) reflect on (humanities terminology) your current topic (appeal to relevance): rites of passage (concretisation) by playing a game (motivation) of *Just a minute*."

"Wossat?"
"Wot?"
"Never 'eard of it"
"Is it *Connect 4* – why can't we play *Connect 4*?"
"It's a well-known Radio 4 panel game and is very funny," I said lamely.
"What's Radio 4?" said Shaun.
"Well, all you have to do is to talk for one minute on the given topic without hesitating or repeating a single word," I replied without taking up the challenge of explaining Radio 4.
"What for?" said Shaun and gave Gary a nudge in the ribs.
"It is educational, interesting, a real challenge and can be fun," I said and immediately asked one of the other teams to get started before any more questions came my way.
"So, let's get this straight," said Emily, sizing up the opportunities, "I have got to talk about this 'rites of

passage' topic for one minute without hesitating or repeating a word."

"That's right."

"And the topic is 'Confirmation'"

"Yes."

"OK, so here goes. Er, Confirmation.." and then Tamsin interrupted.

"You hesitated. You said, er and that's hesitating. So you're out. Ner ner ne ner ner."

"No I didn't," said Emily. "I was just clearing my throat, and that's not hesitating is it, sir?"

I now understood how Nicholas Parsons had felt every week on Radio 4. I had always thought he had a cushy job, but now understood that it wasn't quite so much plain sailing.

"Look," I said despairingly, "I think we'll let Emily have another go as it is her first time. And before anyone could object I said: "Right, Emily, I'll be the referee with the stopwatch, three two one, go."

"Well, Confirmation," she began confidently, "that's when you go to church and the bishop pours water on your head, then one exchanges rings with a bride, next makes some vows, sing a few carols next to the crib, then the Holy Spirit comes and parents give Easter eggs and godparents pay lots of money into your bank account and you wave palms and get a lighted candle in an orange with bits of cloves stuck in and you put cauliflowers and tins of beans and beetroot round the altar to remember when Jesus went to heaven (or was it hell – don't matter – he went somewhere) and babies wear christening robes and aunties all cry and then you have a big party and everyone says you are old enough to get drunk now and it's legal. How long was that?"

She had taken only 30 seconds but everyone was so gobsmacked by this recitation of the Christian calendar in record time that no-one had the courage to say she had repeated "and" and "then" and "the".

"Well done," I said not very convincingly. "Let's now move on to the listening exercise. Ms Postlethwaite wants you to listen to this famous piece of inspiring music and then to draw a picture about what various religions tell us about the meaning of life."

I moved over to the cassette player and was relieved to notice out of the corner of my eye that the class were settling down. They liked drawing. All classes liked drawing and labelling. In fact the whole curriculum for a large number of pupils in the second form*   (*what's your problem?) consisted in drawing and labelling. And colouring in. And copying. Except it was dressed up in far more complex language like: study in depth one particular genre and produce an extended creative think piece using appropriate artistic conventions as illustrative background.

When the class were settled and with their crayons and felt tips at the ready I pressed "Play."

Immediately a loud shriek emanated from the cassette player and the sound of **the Sex Pistols** screaming *"God save the queen"* reverberated around the room. The sound was deafening and I noticed far too late that the volume control was on maximum. I rushed for the cassette player and managed to turn it off before the class had recovered from a universal sense of shock. One or two girls were crying, others had covered up their ears and Shaun and Gary were having fits of laughter.

"Right," I said, "I think we have had enough of that for today. Put down your crayons and get started on your homework. We won't have any more team games today. You can work on your own. You must write a poem. The title is "What is the meaning of life?"

And I thought I might have a go at that myself.

Chapter 10

Summertime

August. Where do teachers go in August? How can life have any purpose when there are no lessons to prepare, no books to mark, no pupils to teach? What is there to do when there is no meeting, no coaching, no mentoring? How to act without a bell, a tannoy, a buzzer prompting their every move? Above all, how to cope without being able to moan about the Head to sympathetic colleagues for a whole month?

August. A time to take stock and a time to unwind; a time for holidays and a time to regroup. A time to look back on the past year and a time to prepare for the next year. A time to renew a subscription for the TES with a new resolve to move to a new school, a new town, a new job.

April may be the cruellest month, but August comes a close second. The unfulfilled plans and dreams of the previous year are there to be contemplated and autumn is just around the corner. It lies between the might-have-beens and should-have-dones and the got-to-get-organised and the things-to-do.

Above all, August is a time for results. All those lessons planned and taught, all those revision sessions and tutorials, all those tears mopped up and encouragements given boil down to just one thing: a grade, a mark, a letter. Early on in the month come the A levels, the gold standard paraded before the nation as the last bulwark against the ever-rising tide of illiteracy and ignorance. The pass rate has gone up! More students than ever are achieving A grades! The girls are seen dancing and hugging and shrieking with joy with their buff envelopes and their glittering grades promising a bright future of academic glory; the boys smirk in the background with their other grades and contemplate a vocational future, a training place, possibly a job and staying at home a little bit longer.

Just as the enthusiasm and the questioning and the soul searching after the A level results (and their bastard son, the A/S levels, tagging along behind) have calmed down, then comes the wave upon wave of GCSEs striding up the garden path to take their place. More pictures of girls weeping and grinning and envelope clutching, more stories of 12 grade A*s, no 14 grade A*s, now here is an eight year old boy with 17 grade A*s (and a C in French), and just as many articles about the dumbing down of grades and the levelling out of results.

Can the pupils of today pass the O levels of yesterday? Do they know their times tables? Can they spell "necessary" and "accommodation" and know the rhyme "Thirty days hath September…" and remember all the colours of the rainbow?

Just because they can listen to an iPod, download a podcast, keep up to date with Twitter, Facebook and several other social networking sites, reply to emails and texts, check out websites, download some tunes and movies, know precisely where their team is in the league and how many points they need to avoid relegation with five away fixtures remaining, eat some pizza and fix a drink, follow the plot of several soaps and know who or what is in and who or what is definitely not in, *all simultaneously,* doesn't prove a thing.

Education has been my life. I was taught, instructed, initiated, educated, coached, trained, informed, drilled, tested, assessed, examined, tutored, schooled, edified, enlightened, guided, improved, and lectured for nearly twenty years and have taught, instructed, initiated, educated, coached, trained, informed, drilled, tested, assessed, examined, tutored, schooled, edified, enlightened, guided, improved and lectured for thirty-eight years.

I have had my mind broadened, my eyes opened, and been shown the ropes; I have been put on the right track and had my wits sharpened; I have been given directions, crammed with facts and stuffed with knowledge; it has been knocked into my head, drilled into me, drummed into my skull. I have been disciplined, broken in, harangued, set tasks and targets.

During six decades I have experienced all that the English education system could throw at me – from nervous and fidgety primary school child, through equally timid and hopeful grammar schoolboy, through wide-eyed and novice university student to postgraduate student teacher, and from there to experienced teacher, teacher trainer, researcher and author, training courses provider and freelance consultant.

I have taken more tests than are good for any human soul: it started with birth certificate (with honours) just in case there was any doubt, then certificate of baptism (Methodist), swimming badge 10 yards, sewing badge, diving certificate (springboard only), music grade 1 (failed), Boys Brigade badges for "Being Helpful", "Good Reader", "Bible Knowledge", Junior School Road Safety certificate, cycling proficiency, motorcycling proficiency (provisional certificate), 11+, O levels, 2nd XI cricket colours and 2nd XI hockey colours, certificate of confirmation (Church of England – free transfer), Heaf test, BCG, chest X-rays, CCF bugle badge, CCF marksman's badge (they must have been kidding surely), Use of English (failed after getting writer's block in exam), A levels (3 – assorted), map reading (passed after cheating), S level (Unclassified – I couldn't translate *"what will not menials do?"* into French – still can't), first degree (with honours) , eye test, driving test, certificate in education, cricket coaching certificate, marriage certificate, First Aid – part 1 (know all about emergency tracheotomies but not how to put on a plaster), IT for dummies, Health & Safety (Part 1), masters degree, blood test, bodily fluid samples in varying quantities,

CRB check, wine appreciation (level 1), and have administered more tests than are healthy: (O levels / A levels / A/O levels / 16+ / GCSE / PGCE / MA assessments).

How to sum up sixty years of contact with the world of education? What have I learned? What can be neatly distilled?

1950s – the primary school experience

If I were to mention that during the first five years of my life there were still ration books, we had no TV and Churchill was prime minister for a good part of that time, which decade would you put me in?

As one of the baby-boomer generation, life during the 1950s seemed a lot less complicated than today. You went to school in order to learn useful things – like reading, writing, times tables and an enduring sense of deference to authority – and there were basic assumptions about each stage in the process.

Primary school prepared you for the 11+ which would determine a future academic path at grammar school for those who passed and a future to escape from for those who failed.

My primary school was a fairly typical red brick building just off the main road, with a small asphalt playground. I remember the playground well because we seemed to spend an inordinate amount of time in it. It was square shaped with a brick wall all around it. The wall regularly had goalposts chalked on one side and there were three stumps chalked on the other side. When not flicking cards, playing marbles, kicking a tennis ball, playing cricket with a tennis ball and bat, or just running around, we would huddle together in corners trying to keep out of the way of larger children.

Education was less about the three Rs and more about the three Cs – crowds, control and cunning. My daily concern was not so much about whether I could remember my spellings or times tables, but whether I could survive being squashed by the bigger boys, avoid the relentless control of the teachers or survive on my wits in all the daily battles over dinner money, milk rations and where I was supposed to be sitting.

I used to take a satchel to school. In this small brown satchel I carried all that was necessary for my education: some string, a fountain pen, a bottle of blue Quink, a blunt pencil, a small box of crayons, a rubber, a (wooden) ruler (inches only of course), my exercise books (ruled), marbles, cards for flicking against the playground wall, a conker or two, some fruit pastilles, a compass and a set of protractors (usually in a little tin box), a game of Owzthat! (two metal hexagonal shapes for playing table cricket that kept many a boy amused throughout interminable lessons – also in a tiny blue metal box). I also had a small English dictionary and (most useful of all) Collins Junior Cyclopedia and Atlas.

This latter book probably started my love affair with trivia and set me on the path to pub quiz bore in later life.

Inside the classroom we had wooden desks with lids and ink holders in the top right hand corner. We used fountain pens and had to use blue ink (usually Quink) with which we filled the pens practically every day. The desks came in pairs and had built-in seats where you would inevitably get a splinter on the back of your legs because we boys all wore short trousers. They were not shorts, but short trousers – a grey flannel material that became very heavy when wet.

Short trousers were a sign of boyhood. We wore them winter and summer with long grey socks and sensible black lace-up shoes. For some reason that I have never quite fathomed, boys' knees had to be exposed to the elements all year round. Quite how this prepared us for adult life I will never know.

Girls wore sensible seersucker dresses. Usually blue.

That's all I can remember about girls at primary school. They didn't like flicking cards or Owzthat!, or marbles, or running around much. Did lots of skipping though.

I did not discover girls again until 1968.

I do not recall being beaten at primary school but that was more than made up for during the next stage of my schooling.

These are the four most important things that I learned whilst at primary school:

1. Milk left by a radiator all morning tastes foul at break time.

2. Polio can be beaten by a sugar cube and a little drop of medicine.

3. A coloured sticker at the end of one's work is the greatest happiness in the whole world.

4. Teachers know everything.

1960s – grammar school pupil and university student.

The 1960s that I experienced were not quite the same that many celebrity memoirs seem to extol. Freewheeling liberal-minded and experimental fashions in music, clothes and behaviour did not percolate down to me or my school.

Short trousers continued right through the first year at my boys only grammar school. And a cap. And a tie (showing the colour of your house). And a blazer (with the house colour around the edge).

Being a first generation grammar school boy during the 1960s was a chastening experience. Having no understanding of arcane ritual nor knowledge of what was expected of me, I quickly learned many things:

- What you know is not as important as who you know.
- Being keen to do well at sport is not as important as having a mother on the PTA.
- Teachers are able to beat you in all manner of ways for not knowing things that they should have taught you in the first place.
- Success is not for the individual pupil but for the glory of the school.
- Girls are a different race.
- Anyone not going to university is regarded as a failure.

Most of the first three years were spent in yearning to fit in and be accepted by my peers. I wanted to please and I wanted to be successful, but did not really know how to achieve either. I can still see that small 12 year old staring out of the Geography class window on a Thursday morning. I was not day dreaming, nor was I watching the world go by. I was watching out for the moment when the PE teacher would post the names of the cricket / hockey teams on the notice board on the other side of the playground. I desperately wanted to be in the team, to belong. It would never be First XI of course, but Second XI or even Third XI would be enough.

Week after week I would be disappointed. I would rush down after the lesson and adopt a deceptively casual air as I made my way to the notice board to take a brief look at the names. I could tell in an instant if my name was present. After all, my name is short and to the point and would appear conspicuous amongst the double-barrelled (Huffington-Smythe) and the one day to be famous (Woolmer). Clutching at straws, I would allow myself to cast my eyes down to the bottom of the list and see if I was named as First Reserve or Twelfth Man. If I was, then I would spend the next two days wishing all kinds of illnesses and misfortunes to befall the names above me so that I could scrape into the team.

If, as occasionally happened, my name actually did appear as one of the chosen XI, I would wander around with an air of smug satisfaction. It was not as though I ever achieved very much on the playing field – I was more likely to drop the crucial catch, get out for a duck or miss an open goal – but at least I was in the team, one of the boys, having that shared experience of togetherness. Getting changed in the pavilion, being in on the team talk, having the team tea, singing on the coach – all these things mattered and gave me a sense of identity and when I was left out, dropped or simply ignored, I felt an overwhelming sense of rejection and isolation.

Being in the team, belonging, having a sense of identity, not being the odd one out, being accepted – all of these emotions and drives and ambitions filled my waking hours and formed my motivation. Unknowingly, in those formative years, I was preparing for my later study of Sartre and Camus. Little did I know then that my later fascination for 20th Century French literature had its roots in the longing of a small boy to play cricket. It came as no surprise to me when I later found out that Camus had been a footballer and Samuel Beckett was the only Nobel Literature laureate to feature in Wisden. *Waiting for Godot* took me right back to that Geography class on a Thursday morning.

At the age of 15 I was considered sane enough to be able to fire bullets. Real bullets. On a firing range. My fellow pupils and I joined the Combined Cadet Force (CCF) in another form of aping of the public schools. National Service had been abandoned in 1960 but it was still clearly felt that it would be useful if a bunch of 15 year olds were able to train with old .303 rifles just in case the Second World War broke out again.

I had no idea what the thinking behind the CCF really was but we all joined in and on one afternoon a week we played toy soldiers. It was all taken very seriously and Geography teachers suddenly became Major Smithers and French teachers became Captain Peters. Prefects were all sergeants and could order us about and shout at us – and even beat us if they wished – and there were other ranks according to age and seniority.

This was 1965. The Vietnam War was beginning to take hold and for the next few years would take the USA down a disastrous route. Race riots were spreading throughout the USA as well. Bob Dylan and Joan Baez and the Beatles and the Rolling Stones dominated the pop charts. A few years after the Cuban missile crisis and with Labour in power, Barry McGuire's *Eve of Destruction* summed up the Zeitgeist.

And from the age of 15 to 18 I marched around in an ill-fitting and uncomfortable khaki uniform, adorned with various badges to show stages of promotion from private to sergeant (although never made prefect), skills in map reading (though I cheated in the exam and to this day cannot read a map), first aid ("burns cannot be treated in the field") and bugling. Quite how I became a bugler remains a mystery. I really wanted to be a drummer, but that was reserved for those who knew the right people and who had parents in the right places, so bugling it was.

I could just about play Reveille and Last Post, but when it came to marching as well as playing the bugle I merely pretended.

We spent a lot of time marching up and down the tennis courts being harangued by older boys. They shouted at us. They swore at us. They occasionally kicked or hit us. This was all exceptionally normal and no-one thought to complain. We all simply looked forward to the following year when it would be our turn and we could inflict the same treatment on younger pupils following us.

This almost seems to be a universal constant in education. I learn through what is said and done to me and I then say and do the same to others. Coupled with a desperate desire to conform to the peer group, not to be different and to please one's elders, it was a formula for fear, compliance and complacency and it worked very well.

What was later termed the *hidden curriculum* was all too clear: conformity to a set of rules laid down by others and to be adhered to without question; obedience; acceptance of casual brutality as part of the norm; mindless drilling for no purpose other than to rob us of any individuality or creativity.

It is said that such cadet forces instil a sense of belonging, pride, patriotism, self-worth, discipline and one can also learn skills that will be useful in later life.

Bollocks.

Skills that I learned through three years in the CCF:

- How to swear
- How to march up and down and do "eyes right" without falling over
- How to shoulder arms
- How to cheat in map reading exams (sit next to your friend and bribe him with chewing gum)
- How to fire a .303 rifle
- How to clean a .303 rifle using a "4 by 2"

- How to clean boots with spit and polish
- How to clean the brass parts of a belt with Brasso without smudging
- How to play a few notes on a bugle
- How to fire a bren gun at a firing range
- How to almost get killed as a 15 year old putting up targets behind the butts at a firing range whilst live ammunition was used
- How to fire blanks on night manoeuvres

Other things that I learned:

- Do what you are told and never question authority
- Bigger people can hit you and get away with it (especially in uniform)
- As I rose through the ranks from private to sergeant I could also mete out punishments, shout at people and strut around like a little Hitler

For a whole term I was put in charge of the school arsenal. On my own. Every CCF afternoon that term I would have to issue .303 rifles to the cadets and then count them back in. In between times I was supposed to clean the rifles and keep the arsenal tidy.

It was just as well that the UK did not have a terrorist threat in the mid-1960s because I don't think that I could have put up much resistance to a dedicated group if they had attacked the arsenal. Anyway, they would probably have found it deserted as it was next to the tuck shop and I spent most of the afternoon in there.

I can honestly say that I have not used any of the so-called skills in later life that I was supposed to have learned in the CCF.

I gained an abiding dislike of the military and a complete suspicion of all forms of authority.

I learned to loathe bullies and recognised that the process itself can turn people into just such bullies – and although at the time I probably didn't recognise it, I feel ashamed of my own bullying tendencies that came to the fore just because I had three little stripes on my arm.

I have never used a weapon since that time and would not have to faintest idea how to anyway.

I dislike the sound of the bugle intensely and can only just stand the trumpet.

I can still remember the taste of hard tack and jam and if I ever tasted it again the Proustian memories of standing up to my knees in a bog at Otterburn Camp whilst on night manoeuvres would come flooding back and I would break down and cry.

What a waste of time.

If only my parents had been scout leaders, or even on the PTA, I could have escaped all that military nonsense and learned to ging-gang-goolie-goolie with the rest of them instead.

In fact only about 3% of my generation went to university – and if you tell the young 'uns that today, they simply don't believe you.

I went to university.

I graduated.

I was now ready to teach.

Or so I thought.

1970s – the student / student teacher / beginning teacher / teacher

So what makes a teacher? How had thirteen years of schooling, three years of university, one year as a foreign language assistant and one year of a post-graduate certificate in education prepared me to teach?

Two things are clear:
(1) It was definitely a certificate in education. The concept of *training* teachers did not infect universities until the early 1990s.

(2) I was expected to teach. I was not expected to *deliver a curriculum*.

We were expected to teach our subject and the pupils were expected to learn it.

When I look back now on what we did during my PGCE year, I cannot but be swallowed up in nostalgia and incredulity. The majority of those on my course had followed a similar path to myself. We had been to grammar schools and we wanted to teach. We had not had experience in any other profession or business and we were mostly in our early twenties. We were believers in comprehensive education, mixed-ability teaching, and education as a good thing in itself.

The course was designed to give us an enjoyable year musing on various philosophies of education, extracts of sociology and psychology and general literature. We saw a number of films, including *Kes, The Prime of Miss Jean Brodie, If.* We had lectures, discussion groups, and some tutorials. We were set about three essays on general topics. The whole of the first term was spent at the university with an occasional day visit to a school.

The second term was spent on teaching practice.

During the third term we were back at the university where we could take options such as sports coaching, music and drama, organising field trips.

Throughout the year there was a general assumption that we all knew what teaching was, we knew our subject matter well and we all knew how children learned. No one questioned these false assumptions and we had virtually no guidance in matters such as behaviour management, assessment and objective-led lesson planning. The reason was that these terms had not then been invented.

The preparation for a career in teaching was in essence a pleasant diversion in the style of the upbringing of a 19th century gentleman. There was to be nothing so gross as discussing the realities of the classroom, nothing so crude as the use of resources and nothing so contemptible as the consideration of pay. Teaching was a calling, a vocation and the idea of ambition was anathema.

It was not surprising therefore that many of us found ourselves in the mould of missionaries out to convert the natives in far off lands when first faced with a class of recalcitrant teenagers. All we had to fall back on was wit, cunning and instinct because our lessons very quickly disintegrated before our eyes.

We also learned many survival techniques and ways of supporting each other by passing on tips from more experienced front line veterans, such as:

Don't smile until Christmas
Never let them smell your fear
Make sure you are never too far from the door
Don't sit in the Head of History's chair

Chapters 1 to 10 outline my life as a foreign language assistant, beginning teacher in Germany, probationary teacher and teacher.

And so the lessons learned as a short-trousered, nervous, uncertain, desperate to please, yearning to succeed, hopeful and often disappointed primary schoolchild seem just as relevant fifty years on:

1) Milk left by a radiator all morning tastes foul at break time.

There are some unpalatable truths that cannot be hidden. Experience is often a truer guide to life than theory.

2) Polio can be beaten by a sugar cube and a little drop of medicine.

Small steps can have significant outcomes.

3) A coloured sticker at the end of one's work is the greatest happiness in the whole world.

What is your coloured sticker?

4) Teachers know everything.

If only they could teach it.

And so I come full circle.

Still in TA. Still sometimes in denial. Still sometimes relapsing. Still striving. Best be still. Sit still. Still or sparkling. Stand still. The still of the night. Still photograph. Still your fears. Be still and know. Still born. Stay still. Still small voice. Still life. Stille Nacht. Still waters. Still yearning.

Still crazy after all these year's.